Absence of Light

Ryan's Story

Before The Light #2

Absence of Light (Ryan's Story)
Before the Light #2
By
Melyssa Winchester

Copyright © 2014 Melyssa Winchester

This is a work of fiction. Names; characters; places and incidents are the products of the author's imagination or are used fictitiously. Any resemblance to actual events, locales or persons living or dead is entirely coincidental.

Cover Image Copyright: Karelnoppe @ Dreamstime and Teresa Yeh @ Dreamstime
Cover Image Design: Melyssa Winchester

"Never think about something wrong you did in the past. Always look forward with your head high. Have no regrets."
– Jared Leto

Prologue
Back Where It All Began

"Idle hands are the devil's playthings."

Serenity has been missing for over a month and despite my claims to the contrary, there is nothing but truth in the above statement. I've been doing everything I can to keep myself grounded. Keeping the darkest part of me buried as deeply I can, going so far as to stay away from everything that could be seen as a temptation, but it doesn't help. I can feel myself slipping.

In moments of absolute quiet, like what I find myself in now, I'm forced to remember things better left forgotten. A time in my life that I wish I could just close my eyes and will away. It's something I can never do, though, and as the memories are starting to prove, it isn't just one particular time in my life I want to banish.

It's all of it.

At least the life I lived before Serenity Richards became a part of it. Before I was given the one gift I never thought I was worthy of.

The light.

You see, I'm not your average guy. I might be able to walk and talk like one, even look like one, but buried deep, there is so much that will always separate me from every other person walking the planet.

I'm not one of them. I'm not one of *you*.

Wait, that's not coming out right. Let me start over.

I'm human. For the most part. I was born to a human mother and lived in the same house my entire life. I did the same things every other kid on the block did, but there's something living inside me that isn't visible with anyone else.

I'm part demon.

I know what you're thinking. This guy's completely lost his mind and honestly, I don't blame you for thinking that way. I wish this was me making up a bunch of horseshit and feeding it to you But the reality is, there isn't a damn bit of this that's made up or part of some elaborate ruse designed to pull the wool over your eyes.

I am what I've admitted to being. No matter how much I wish it wasn't true and that things had happened differently. That I wasn't placed in the position I am now.

Having to remember a life that I never should have been forced to life, and attempting to come to terms with the damage that life caused the rest of the world.

*****

It started when my mom decided she was sick and tired of being lonely and went trolling at the bar. A decision that cost her and eventually me any chance at a normal existence.

That night she'd been determined to head out with a few of her girlfriends, get drunk off her ass, meet some random guys and end the night hooking up with one of them. She did what she set out to do, but by the end of the night, got a whole lot more than she bargained for.

Enter Daemon, my sperm donor. Or the way the rest of the world views it, my father.

To hear Corinne tell it, he appeared like any other human guy would. He chatted her up for a while, eventually pulling her away from her friends and getting her to focus her attention solely on him. I'm pretty sure knowing my mom, it wasn't that hard for him to do. She never did have much of an attention span, which means I have no doubt that when faced with a guy that looks the way my father did, she had *no* issue at all walking away from her friends for one on one time with him.

As she predicted before she even got to the bar, she ended up spending the night with Daemon. It was only in the early hours of the morning that she learned just who she'd laid down with.

Most would think that learning that you spent the night with a demon, would be enough to scare you off, but most people aren't my mom. Instead of running, she embraced it. That's where it all started, but I didn't realize it until years later. By embracing Daemon so easily, she had decided my fate before I even came into existence.

In an attempt to appear to be the best damn demon lover she could be, my mother invited her paramour to live with her, accepting that he would need to be in and out at all hours and would sometimes bring unsavory people and things home in an effort to feed the hunger that lived inside him.

For a while, according to her, it worked. Daemon came and went as he pleased and she put up with it. At least she did until the day she found out she was pregnant with me.

My old man's free ride had come to an end now that there was going to be a new mouth to feed. She expected things of him that most human men can't even live up to. As much as I hate him, I gotta say, he did the right thing splitting, demon or not. It's half the reason I did the same thing when Lucifer came for me.

Living with my mother was not easy. No matter how hard anyone tried, her unrealistic expectations were too much even for the most powerful demon in hell.

I don't remember much of the early years, only having her ramblings and Lucifer's memories to go on, but it seems that right from the minute she pushed me out, she hated me. People speak of living in hellholes. Well I can honestly say, I had my first experience living in one before I was even born. Corinne McGregor didn't have a mothering bone in her body and even now, twenty-three years later, she still doesn't.

According to Lucifer, the minute she was given the okay to bring me home, he watched over me because he didn't trust Corinne and after everything I've learned, I can see why. At first I thought he watched over me because he knew he would use me, but that wasn't the case. If he wanted to use me he was going to have to make sure that I lived long enough for it to happen and with my mom and her hatred, that wasn't a guarantee.

Corinne, she was a smoker. It's one of the first memories I have of her as a little kid. She always had one of those cancer sticks hanging from her lips. What I didn't know was that practically from the time she brought me through the front door, she was using those smokes to burn me. At first it wasn't anything intentional, just ashes falling as she was feeding me, but as time went on, she physically put them to my skin, making sure I knew, even as a baby that I was a mistake and not wanted.

I'd like to say it got better with time, but let's face it, I'm a half demon for a reason. There's a reason that when Lucifer finally came for me at fifteen, I took off like someone lit a fire under my ass.

Living with Corinne, it never got better. All she could see was Daemon. What he was, what he put her through with everything she willingly accepted from him, and most of all, she saw his leaving. I was a constant reminder of what she had lived through and in the end lost and she was determined right from the very first day to never let me forget it.

I'm not supposed to exist. I'm not saying that because my mom wishes I was never born. I'm saying it because it's fact.

When a demon lies down with a human, there has never been a documented case of a child being born from it. There's something in the DNA I guess that makes it so that a demon can't ever conceive. Whether it works for the angels in the same way, I suppose I'll eventually learn considering what I am, but a demon, they can't do it. Or they couldn't until the day Daemon was stupid enough to lay down with my mother.

When Corinne announced she was pregnant, Daemon had been the one to tell her that. He had spoken out about her being a harlot, a whore and a woman that despite her claims of love, was stepping out and sleeping around. Considering what he was, I always found this part of her story funny. None the less, he'd told her flat out that I didn't belong to him. Even after I was born and the truth was there in my eyes, he couldn't see past it and believe the truth and up until the day he was finally eradicated, he never did.

They had created something that should not exist.

They created me.

An abomination.

*****

This is the part of being alone that I hate. I'm remembering everything about my life before Serenity blew her way like a hurricane into it. I'm remembering the darkness and when that happens, it brings the hunger and anger to the surface and they fight against the control I've managed to create until it's a constant power struggle to keep myself grounded. I don't want to think about these things, but the longer I spend locked away the way I am, and without her, I've got no choice.

Until Serenity comes back, I'm going to have to live with the constant reminder of the way I was before her, and even what I could be again if for some reason she's never found.

So instead of running from it, swallowing it down and focusing on something as brightly bathed in the light as Serenity is, I'm going to embrace it. Look it dead in the eye and confront it once and for all.

I'm Ryan McGregor, human-demon hybrid and this is my story.

Chapter One
The Beginning

When I think about my life, especially the earlier parts, I have a hard time remembering what happened before I turned four. I can remember a whole hell of a lot after that, most of which I wish I didn't, but it all seems to begin for me then.

Waking up the morning of my fourth birthday, the scent of burnt toast wafting its way up through the vents and straight into my room, I just knew it was going to be a day different than the others. It's not like I woke up expecting my mom to shower me with gifts and her undying love for me. Even at four I knew that the likelihood of that happening was slim to none. The reason that day was different is because of the conversation I walked in on when I finally made my way downstairs.

*****

"Corinne, you are ill equipped to handle the boy. I know what you think of me based on the things you've been told and read, but would you please give some thought to what I have asked?"

"I may not be mother of the year, but there's no way in hell I'm letting the likes of you or even Daemon get your hands on him."

It's not the first time I've heard her like this. She's upset, but the man standing across from her doesn't seem to be at all bothered by it. In fact, the way he's standing, he looks relaxed, almost as if he'd been expecting this to be her response. I'm not sure what he's asking and I don't even know if I get a vote, but whatever he's selling, I'm buying.

I want him to take me away.

"You said yourself that his powers are growing at an alarming rate. One that a being such as yourself cannot keep up with. I do

believe it's time that you give him over to us, so that we may work with him. Nurture the gifts that continue to grow so that one day he can take his rightful place at my side."

"Did you not hear me, Lucifer? Ryan won't be going anywhere with you!"

"I do not need your consent in this matter, Corinne. I am merely here out of respect for your position as the boys' mother. You are aware of what runs in his veins. You merely want to keep him with you so you have an outlet for all of your hate and despite what has been said about me by others, I cannot allow that."

She laughs and I don't understand why. I didn't hear him say anything funny. Who is this man my mom called Lucifer? How does he know us? Better yet, what does he mean by gifts?

"You have no idea what I'm dealing with!"

"That is where you are mistaken. I understand quite well what you are having to endure, just as I understand what the boy himself endures every day being under this roof. You are aware of Daemon's power. It cannot come as a surprise that one born of him would show the same level, even at this young an age."

"Do not speak his name again! I know what he means to you, but where is your precious confidante now? Off screwing his way through half of the city, no doubt. He has done nothing for me—"

"I am afraid I cannot allow you to speak when all that comes out of your mouth is nonsense. This has nothing to do with you, and everything to do with the boy. Or have you forgotten that in your selfishness?"

It's obvious my mom doesn't like the man she's speaking with, but the more he says, the stronger the urge inside of me is to run to him, grab on for dear life and never let go. He has no idea what his being here means. He's my savior. He will take me out of this place and make everything okay again. I just know it.

"It also has nothing to do with Daemon. Yes, he is an integral part of my plans moving forward, but that is all he is. As it pertains to Ryan, Daemon has not nor will he ever have a say."

"He won't have anything to do with this?"

She seems to be softening. Her shoulders, tensed and rigid before are now relaxing with the promise from the man. As long as this Daemon guy isn't involved, it looks like she'll let me go. I've heard all I need to. I'm positive that what's happening is the right thing.

I'm finally going to be able to escape this place and leave the horror behind forever.

"As I have already told you, what I am requesting will benefit the boy and myself only."

"Fine."

"You must excuse my lack of understanding, but what do you mean by fine?"

"Exactly what it sounds like. If you swear to me that this has nothing to do with that demonic asshole you have chosen to be your second in command, and you're here for Ryan, then I'll agree."

I wasted no time the second she said the words, running from my hiding spot in the corner. Hearing my mother giving this man permission to take me away, it was as if Christmas came early. Only this time, instead of a beating or another lashing with the belt, the way it had been the last two years, I was going to get what I wanted.

My escape.

*****

I had no clue at the time who the guy standing in my kitchen was, or even what my mom was agreeing to, but none of that really mattered because there was something I did see and understand.

My way out.

Of course nothing ever comes that easily, at least it doesn't for me. If I had come down a few minutes before, I would have known what he originally asked her. What the plan really was, but because I came into it too late, all I had to go on was half a conversation and a whole lot of assumptions.

Where I thought he was there to save me and take me away, he wasn't. At least not that day. He was making a plan for the time when he would come back in the future. What I didn't realize until much later, is that my mother sold my soul to him in the kitchen that morning. Despite her reservations as they pertained to the man known as my father, she still gave in.

Corinne McGregor really did want to be rid of me and would go to any lengths to do so.

Even when it meant signing me over to the devil.

I'm pretty sure when you're four, the last thing you should be worried about is where your next meal is going to come from, how many guys your mom's gonna come home with, or even if you're going to live to see the sun come up on any given day. That's how my life was though, but I never talked about it. It might have had something to do with my limited vocabulary, but I wouldn't dare speak up about the way things were.

I might not have understood what she was doing in allowing Lucifer to come back for me, but there could be no denial that I would suffer through it until he did because even at that young an age, I knew he was my only way out.

It was also that day, after wrapping my body around him, determined not to let go, that I heard it for the first time.

Up until that point, the only way I would know the horrible things she thought about Daemon and me was if she spoke them out loud, which I do remember her doing more often than not, but that morning was different. There was no movement in her jaw the way you see when most people speak and her lips were pursed in a straight line, but I was able to hear her clear as day. It's only when I looked between the both of them and caught the man's smile beaming down at me that I realized something pretty important was going on.

I could hear her thoughts. I had been shown my first 'gift'.

*****

"Ryan, if you can hear me, you must let me know."

I'm not sure what's going on, but where I heard my mom saying some pretty horrible stuff before, now I can hear him. His head is tilted in my direction and he's smiling, but how he's talking to me, I don't understand.

If what I believe is correct and you can hear me, please focus on a yes or no answer.

I do as he says and I focus everything I have on the word yes. Wanting him to know I can hear him even though his lips still haven't moved and it's kind of scaring me.

"Yes, I hear you."

Judging by the way his face lights up at the words spoken in my mind, I can tell he's heard me. I don't have a whole lot to go on with my mom being angry all the time, but from what I've seen on TV and movies, people are usually pretty happy and smiling when something good happens, the same way he is now.

I am aware of what your life has been like, but I am here to make sure that I put an end to it. When the time is right, I am going to come back for you and when I do, I will take you far away from here and you will never have to return again. I know it is not what you want to hear right now, but it is the best that I can do.

"Why can't you take me with you now?"

Answering him back again, I think I know what's going on. For some reason when this man is around, I'm able to do magic. I can do things that other people can't. I always thought there was more to me, but doing this with Lucifer, I can see that he's put some kind of spell on me so I can talk to him without my mom hearing.

He's a magician.

I assure you, I am not a magician, but if that is what it takes in order for your mind and heart to calm then that is where you must put your focus. I cannot take you now as it is not yet time, but it is my promise that when everything is in order, I will come back. You see, Ryan, you are part of a much bigger plan. None of what comes next can happen without you.

*****

When someone tells you that you're part of a bigger plan, you should pay attention. Even if you're four years old and dying for a little acknowledgement that doesn't have anger attached to it. You should probably pay attention when they tell you that it can't happen without you either.

I didn't do any of that. I ate up every word and accepted it for what I thought it was at the time. He promised he would come back and I believed it. I knew he was speaking the truth. It was another ability of mine, one that until that moment, I hadn't known about. Sensing deception despite the person's best attempt at hiding it.

With his words ringing so much truth, it opened my eyes to all the lies I'd been told up until that point. It was in those moments with him that first time that I started to learn a truth of my own.

I had a purpose after all. I was destined to change the world.

Chapter Two
The Voices

About a year later when I turned five, I noticed the coolest thing.

Well it was the coolest thing until a teacher caught it happening and sent me to the office. It didn't take long after I left class for them to call my mom and tell her something was wrong with my eyes.

You see, that's another part of me that's not quite right. I've got blue eyes, but when I get mad, frustrated or remotely bothered, the black rim that's always been around them, it seems to grow and they turn completely black.

What the school didn't know and what I couldn't get a word in edgewise to tell them, is the absolute worst thing you can do is call my mom when she's at work, and considering what she did for a living, I'm using that term loosely.

She didn't think I knew what all her late nights were about, but trust me, when you've had to make peanut butter sandwiches for dinner thirty days in a row because she's not home until you're already in bed, you start to catch on quick. It's also easy to tell with the revolving door of men that came in and out of our place.

My mother wasn't a bartender, waitress or anything remotely respectable like that. No. Her job was the one thing you could never admit to when you're hanging with your buddies, or the school hosted a career day at school. You know the one. The day where they stand up in front of the class and tell everyone what they do for a living.

She couldn't do that because she was a prostitute. It's another thing she blames on dear old dad. The guy might have been a demon, but I'm pretty sure he didn't force her to sell her body for cash. She did that all on her own and it had nothing to do with us not having enough to get by, or some other reason that the general population might have sympathy for.

My mom just liked to fuck.

The day the school called and told her to come pick me up, she'd decided to take a day shift as well as her regular spot at night. When she showed up at the school, I wanted to run from her. It wasn't often she came there, us living so close I could easily walk myself there and back, but on the rare times she did, she was dressed properly. Not that day.

She had the good sense to put on a pair of pants thankfully, but whatever she'd been in the middle of when she got the call was obvious because she ran into the office with nothing on top but her bra. I know they said it was important that she come, but all I can remember thinking at the time was, couldn't she have taken at least a few minutes to make herself presentable?

It was so wrong.

I've never wanted to leave a place so badly in my life, well, other than home, but my hatred for my home is well documented.

To say she was pissed by the time we got home would be an understatement. The beating she laid on me with not only her belt, but a paddle, won't ever be forgotten even though the bruises faded a long time ago. If she hadn't done it though, I never would have known that the thing with my eyes had been going on for a while.

She told me that day, just like she has every day before it that it was just another thing that was Daemon's fault and it made the hatred she had already unleashed since I'd been born that much worse.

I found myself praying for the man in the kitchen to come back. It had been a little over a year at that point. I was pretty sure that meant it was the right time. If he would just come back and take me away, I wouldn't have to deal with her anymore. He wouldn't hate what my eyes did. In fact, I'm pretty sure with the cool mind trick he showed me, he'd love it.

My thought process at the time was probably even more twisted than it is now and it's no secret the way my life has been blown to shit recently.

The day she picked me up from school, brought me home and proceeded to beat on me, I had reached a point where instead of running the way I used to every time she came at me with that look in her eye, I just took it. I accepted every lashing with the belt, every slam of her fist, all the while focusing on the man's face and wishing with everything I had that he could be my father.

As much as my mom seemed to despise what he had to say the last time he was here, there was a way she looked at him that meant she was scared. So in my mind, if he was my dad, he could use whatever power he had to make sure she was too afraid to touch me.

Too bad life doesn't work that way.

Life went on after the beating that day, but it was never quite the same.

I found myself going out of my way to get mad just so I could see the way my eyes turned black. It became a game to me. I did it so much, I started keeping track of how fast it happened and how often. For a five year old boy with no other outlet, it was seriously the coolest thing ever.

By the time I turned six, with there still being no sign of the man, or even a clue that my silent pleas had been heard, I started to buy into the belief that I'd made him up. I started telling myself that I'd been living with the strain of hatred from my mom for so long that I made him up so I could have something to focus on when things became too hard.

It was right around that time when I learned of another 'gift' I had. Being able to speak in my mind, read my mom's thoughts and even have my eyes change at the drop of a hat wasn't enough. No. There was still a whole lot more to come and this newest one didn't disappoint.

I'm not entirely sure what she was thinking, but my mom went ahead and got me some matchbox cars for this particular birthday and it was during some time playing with them that it happened the first time.

There were always voices in my house, my mom's or one of her many *boyfriends*, but there was something off about this one. Where they always sounded muffled because my door was between whatever they were talking about and what I was doing, this one was clear.

*****

"Please tell Jonathan I forgive him."

Spinning around at the sound, my eyes instantly fall on my closet, wondering if maybe one of my mom's friends found his way in here and is playing some kind of joke on me. It's only when I hear it again, this time coming from behind me that I realize it's something more than just one of mom's friends.

"He needs to know it wasn't his fault. It was my time to go."

"Time to go where?" I ask, not sure why I'm answering, but curious all the same.

"To die of course."

"But I can hear you, so how can you be dead?"

"You must find Jonathan and tell him. He needs to know!"

The voice raises and just like I've heard with my teachers before, I know it's nothing good. Whatever this person thinks I need to tell Jonathan, its super important and they're getting pretty worked up about it. I don't know what I'm supposed to do to help, but it's all I want to do right now. I don't want to hear this voice so upset anymore. It hurts.

"Where does Jonathan live?"

"224 Sycamore Road. You must find him and tell him."

"I'll tell him, I swear!"

I don't know who the voice is or who the guy is, but this is seriously the coolest thing ever. I shoot another look around my room, searching for any sign that there's someone hiding and just waiting for the right time to jump out. Standing up and walking over by my bed, bending down just enough to make sure there's nothing hiding under it, I turn back to the direction I heard the voice speak.

"Who are you?"

"My name is Riley Henderson."

"Hi Riley! I'm Ryan. I just turned six and I got the coolest cars for my birthday. You wanna see?"

Before the voice can answer back, my door cracks and in the time it takes me to blink from the hallway light now flooding into the room, my mom makes her way through.

"Who the hell are you talking to?"

"Riley!"

I can tell by the look on her face that she doesn't believe me, but right now with the way I feel, I could care less what she thinks. I've got a new friend and it's one that the minute I can get out of the house on my own, I'm going to help. I'm gonna make sure I find Jonathan and tell him what she told me.

"Whatever. Just keep it down."

She backs out, closing the door behind her and I'm surrounded by silence. I don't like the quiet very much. It reminds me of how alone I am usually, but everything's different now. I've finally got a friend to talk to.

"Riley, are you still here? If you are, please answer. That was my mom, but she's gone now."

*****

Riley never did answer me back that night, but that was my first taste of speaking with the dead. I had no idea at the time that the voices that would come at all hours were actually dead people, but it made the days go faster, so after a while, I didn't even care who or what they were, as long as they blocked out the crap I had to deal with.

It was also the first and last time that I did something that one of the voices asked me to do. Riley coming to me that night, it might have been the last time I saw her, but it wasn't the last time I spoke about her.

That happened when I finally tracked down Jonathan a few months later.

It wasn't easy, but I did it. I found Jonathan Henderson, Riley's husband, but the reaction I was hoping for when he finally opened the door wasn't at all what I was expecting.

*****

"Can I help you?"

From my place on the step, I can smell him. He smells the way my mom does when she comes home late at night or early in the morning. Cigarettes and alcohol. He smells like he's been bathing in the stuff.

"It's not your fault."

"Excuse me?"

"I'm supposed to tell you that it's not your fault."

He doesn't get it. I can tell by the way his eyes are scrunching in. It's another look I recognize because of how often I see the same one on my mom's face. I'm annoying him.

"Get lost, kid. This ain't funny."

"It's not supposed to be funny. Riley told me to tell you that it's not your fault."

This gets his attention. His body which had been leaning against the door for support, stands up straight, his posture rigid and his eyes which had been mildly annoyed before, look downright scary now. He's angry.

"What the hell you know about Riley?"

"I know she's dead. She told me. She also told me to find you and tell you that it's not your fault."

Where I'd been expecting his eyes to go soft, his body to relax knowing that even with her dead she was still trying to reach out to him, even if it was through a little kid, it doesn't happen.

He steps through the door and instead of being nice to me, shoves me down the steps until my body is crashing against the cold, hard ground below me, his eyes venomous and angry and his lips dipped into a frown.

"Get the fuck out of here kid and if you know what's good for you, don't ever come back."

*****

I did as he said once my body stopped stinging enough to get off the ground and he had gone back into his house, slamming the door behind him. I never went back and with the reaction I'd gotten from Jonathan, I never listened to another voice again.

I'd learned my first lesson that day and it's one that I've held onto every day since. People will never understand the things they can't wrap their minds around and my gift of being able to communicate with the dead was definitely something no one could understand.

It didn't take long after that, with the voices visiting me as often as they were, for my mother to catch on to what was happening. I swear, I started to think that the so called gifts the man spoke of were anything but. It seemed like every time I picked up an ability that I had no control over, my mom lost her mind just a little bit more.

Where she'd been angry at me for existing, it got worse with every new thing I learned. I think she might have tried at one point to look at me like I was similar to everyone else, but the more things that appeared, especially with the way my eyes would change, it became harder for her to believe. She couldn't deny that I was my father's son anymore and it royally pissed her off.

*****

"It doesn't matter what I do, it doesn't change anything! You're exactly like him! It's bad enough that you look like him, do you really have to act like him too?"

"Look like who, Mommy?"

"You know who, Ryan. Your useless, no good, piece of shit father!"

Whenever she raises her voice at me, it's scary. I don't like it. Usually I know what comes when she gets in one of her moods like this, but with the way she's yelling questions at me this time, it's not the same.

"I don't have a daddy, remember? You told me that."

"I don't even know why I bother talking to you like this. You're too stupid to get it. Go to your room and whatever you do, don't take a step out of it for the rest of the night."

I want to reach out to her. She looks like she needs a hug. I've seen people do it on TV all the time. Whenever someone feels bad, all you have to do is hold onto them and the person is made better again. I want to do that so bad for her. Maybe if she had someone to hug, she wouldn't be so mean all the time.

"I love you Mommy."

"What did I tell you? Go to your room! I can't stand the sight of you."

*****

I'm not sure if it was because I was so young or I was more human than I wanted to admit, but that wasn't my last attempt at trying to get through to her. When telling her I loved her never worked and hugs and kisses failed, I began to act out in hopes that eventually I would do something that she couldn't distance herself from and she'd show me that deep down under all that hatred and anger, she loved me back.

The bike incident was probably my best and worst attempt. The funny thing is, I wasn't even trying at that point. When I came home with the gouge in my head though, I had to admit there was this small part of me that thought physical injury might be the way to her heart.

I was such a stupid kid. Naïve to the very end. It didn't work, and honestly the whole incident is like a really bad dream. Where all the other kids in my neighborhood had parents that would come running when something like what I went through happened, my mom didn't even flinch. There was no cleaning of my wounds, no hugs or kisses. There was nothing remotely close to caring that took place at all.

It was the complete opposite.

*****

I open the door slowly, making sure my mom wouldn't hear the old creak that's been there probably as long as I have. My head's pounding and even though it seems like the blood finally stopped, I could feel globs of it at the top of my forehead still. Every once in a while one of them dripping down and making it hard to see.

There was a reason she bought me the pads and the helmet, but she knew me and what I was capable of. There was no way someone like me, that could do the things I could do would ever need it, so when I left the house earlier, I'd left them all behind.

I was such an idiot.

"Ryan, is that you?" She calls from the kitchen and my body tenses. I don't know how she's going to react, seeing me this way. I hoped I could get up to the bathroom and have a bath before she even realized anything was up.

"Yeah, it's me."

With a final look at the stairs, wondering if I should just run up them before she comes out and catches me standing here, I finally move my feet in the direction of the kitchen. Maybe when she sees what I did to myself, she'll be worried and I'll find out she actually cares about me after all. I won't have anything to fear.

It would be a dream come true if she did that, but with each step I take that brings me closer to her, I don't hold out much hope.

The minute she hears my shoes scuffing on the tile, she turns around and as her eyes lock on mine, moving only slightly as she takes in what must be the dried blood in my hair and the tear stains on my cheeks, I feel my heart speed up in anticipation of whatever her reaction's gonna be.

It's only when her body tenses and a scowl comes across her face that I know I've gotten my hopes up for nothing. For a split second before her eyes landed back on mine, they seemed to go lighter, softer even, and now, just as quickly as it appeared, it's gone and I'm face to face with my mother again.

The one that doesn't feel anything.

Corinne the monster.

"What's with the tears? You're a fucking boy for Christ sakes! Start acting like it."

She turns her back before I can answer, and I feel my heart descend deep into my chest the minute she's completely turned around. I've tried every way I can think of to make her see that just because I look like him, I'm not my dad and nothing works. She hates me. She's always going to hate me and not even physically hurting myself is going to change it.

Despite what she said, the tears continue to fall as I turn around and go right back out the way I came. All the while thinking about what she just said to me. What it means and how right she is.

I'm a boy, and boys aren't supposed to cry. They're supposed to be strong, never letting on that they feel anything. If that's what she thinks I need to do, then it's what I better do. All I'm doing crying like this is proving to her what a good little girl she's raised.

Wiping the remainder of the tears away as I reach the stairs, I climb them one at a time, all the while trying to ignore the pounding taking place in my head and the ache that's threatening to rip a hole through my chest.

If my mom wants a boy, then that's exactly what she's going to get. I'm never going to let on that I feel anything ever again.

It's what a good boy does.

*****

The one thing she hated most about me was how similar I was to Daemon. I looked like him, had a lot of the same mannerisms, and as she told me before, the same abilities. What she didn't realize then and probably still doesn't now, is that it was that hatred for me that started the transition.

I stopped feeling altogether that day, never once shedding another tear or giving a damn about anything. It wasn't because I'm a half demon hybrid, or even that my father was a demon that did it.

It was her.

She neglected me and twisted me up so much that she shoved me straight at the darkness she embraced so easily years before.

Corinne brought the demon to life and nothing was ever going to be the same again.

Chapter Three
Say A Little Prayer

By the time my eighth birthday rolled around, I'd done what I set out to do. I didn't display any emotion whenever I interacted with my mother. Hell, I didn't even do it at school. I kept away from all the other kids, though that was mainly because the minute they saw me talking to myself, they booked it pretty fast in the other direction.

I didn't care. I didn't need anyone. Least of all some stupid kids who thought they were the only thing in life that mattered. Fighting each other tooth and nail to be the center of attention. Each one more important than the last.

I'm the first to tell you that not allowing yourself to feel or care about anything, is a lonely existence. As much as I was used to being on my own and liking it, it still didn't mean I didn't ache for something more. Want to experience what it really was to feel something besides loathing and hatred.

Want to be something different and better than the role model that I'd been left with.

It was around that time that I gave up on the man known as Lucifer ever returning. It had been so long by then that even remembering the conversation he had with my mother that day was hard. The longer he stayed away, the more I forgot about him and the more it appeared as though it was something my mind conjured up after all.

I wanted to believe in what he promised me, but with each passing day I lost a little more hope. Days bled together, the same routine taking place seemingly on repeat until I found myself just rolling with the sameness of it all.

The voices had reached an all-time high by this point. I heard them everywhere I went. What started out as only one quickly became multiple ones at the same time, until they all blended together making it hard as hell to keep up with them.

Some wanted help, others wanted to complain, and then there were the ones that made no sense at all. They all came together like a jumble in my head. I learned over time not to speak to them out loud, but it still didn't lessen how often I heard them or the nauseated way I would feel after they'd grown tired and finally left me alone.

The first time one appeared to me at school, I had no idea that talking back to it openly would be considered weird. As soon as I heard the voice, I answered it, and without thinking, sealed my fate for what was the rest of my academic life. People gave me strange looks in the hall, threw things on me when they thought I wasn't looking and treated me like a pariah.

What they didn't realize, was they were only treating me the way I already felt. I knew I was different, having abilities that nobody else had, so the way they acted toward me was only them doing to me what I couldn't do to myself.

I was a freak, so it made sense to be treated like one. I accepted what the world now calls bullying the way I seemed to accept everything else.

I'd had enough by the time I turned eight, though. I needed relief. I wanted there to be someone else out there in the world like me. More than that, I wanted to find them so that going through everything wouldn't be nearly as hard. If someone was there by my side, walking me through everything I was experiencing, I knew I would be able to get through it that much easier.

The sad reality is, no matter how much I searched to find this person, they never appeared. The longer I went without finding someone like me, the more I began to believe I was alone in this. I really was the abomination my mother continued to tell me I was.

I thought the way most outcasts do, but I didn't realize it at the time because I was so young. I really believed there was no way out. I was stuck this way forever.

If you knew the way my mom felt about this sort of thing, you'd know that what I did next, she would have seriously lost her shit over if she'd ever found out about it. Unable to handle the loneliness, I did the unthinkable, at least as far as she's concerned and considering what I believed about myself even then, it was pretty unthinkable for me too.

You see, it doesn't take a brain surgeon to realize that the woman that laid down with a demon wasn't the most religious person on the planet. Growing up, all I ever heard was how anything remotely related to God was crap. Even before she met Daemon, she was against it. It just got a whole lot worse after what happened with my old man. Add in having me and well, you can see what would happen if I spoke out about anything remotely related to church or religion. She would have strung me up by my balls.

One night when the ache was too much and the voices wouldn't let up, I did the only thing left I could do. I'd seen from watching television and hearing other people's conversations that it worked, so it was my last ditch attempt at getting what I needed so badly.

I prayed.

From what I can remember from the movies I watched and books I read, when you pray, some believe it goes directly to the big man himself, while others believe that the silent plea of your heart goes to the angels. I gotta say that at eight I didn't really give much thought to who would be answering. All I knew was that I wanted it answered.

The night it happened was just like every other one. I went to school, walked myself home and made myself something to eat for dinner. I spent some time alone in my room, playing with the three year old Matchbox cars and doing what I figure most kids do in using my imagination to make it more fun. It's only when the voices interrupted my play time that I finally broke down and found myself kneeling over my bed the way I'd seen a little boy do in a book I read.

Putting my hands together as tightly as I could and closing my eyes, only opening them every few seconds to make sure no one could hear or see me, I focused my mind and let everything just come pouring out.

Hi. My name is Ryan McGregor, and I need some help. I know you must be super busy, but I don't know who else to ask. My mom doesn't like you much, so if she knew I was doing this, I'd probably get the belt again, but if you do give me what I want, I'd gladly take my whooping because I'd be so happy.

Are there other people like me in the world? If there is, do you think if I swear to be really good, you can send one to me? I don't like being the only one who can hear voices. I don't like that I'm the only one that can read everyone's thoughts when I don't even know what I'm thinking half the time. I don't want to feel so alone. If you're too busy, it's okay if you don't answer, but this is the only thing I want. I won't ask you for another thing ever, I swear. I hope you hear this and can help.

I don't want to be alone anymore.

I'm not sure what I was expecting, but I do remember being pretty damn disappointed when nothing happened in the moment. I guess I expected that if other people had their prayers answered, then mine would be instantaneous. I mean who could deny a little kid, right?

It didn't stop there. I prayed more than that. I swear by the time I turned nine, I must have sent that prayer and ones just like it up about three hundred times. I left class during the day in order to send a short one up while standing in the stall of the boy's bathroom. I prayed silently on my walks home every day and before bed every night. Anytime things became too much, I was sending up a prayer. The fact that I might have been overloading Heaven with how often I was doing it never even entered my mind.

Just when I gave up all hope of ever hearing anything from God or even the angels, something happened, or rather someone entered my life that brought it all back again.

Up until that point, my school day consisted of getting there about ten minutes before the bell rang, walking around the yard alone, taking in everything around me and doing everything in my power to block the voices. I would travel from one class to the next, not paying attention to anyone or anything going on around me. It was my ultimate goal just to make it through the day with no issues.

With me not having any friends, I would use time in between classes to do homework and eat whatever random lunch I managed to put together for myself and complete the afternoon much the way I did the morning. I would leave school the minute the bell rang and begin the walk back home.

It was that same repeated cycle every day, with no real deviation, until he showed up.

Jackson Bryant transferred in about halfway through the year and for whatever reason, the kids did nothing to embrace him. He got treated horribly right from the start and even now, years later, I have no idea why that happened. Needless to say, because of the way we were both treated, we seemed to latch on to one another pretty quickly once we finally interacted.

I don't make friends easily. I hate most people if you want to get to the heart of it, but I was different with Jackson. Maybe it's because he was being tormented the same way I was even though there was nothing about him that set him apart from everyone else. Whatever the reason, he came up to me about two weeks after he got there, plopped himself down on the grass beside me and he never left.

At least not right away.

*****

"Hey! You mind if I sit with you?"

I'd seen the shadow of the person before actually getting a good look at who it was, but now that I knew it wasn't someone intent on dumping their lunch all over me, I just shrugged in response. I knew this guy, he was in pretty much all my classes, but it was the first time he'd interacted with me, aside from the grunting he did when he needed to get past me in the hall.

"So is everyone that goes here an asshole or is it just our class?"

I'm familiar with cursing. My mom is the queen of it, but I can't say I've heard it a lot here at school. I think there's a fear in getting caught that keeps most kids from saying what deep down I just know they're dying to say.

It doesn't seem to be a problem for Jackson though.

"It's everyone. The school's full of jerks."

"Great." He moans before sticking his hand out across the grass. "I'm Jackson."

Never spending much time with other kids my age, him sticking his hand out freaks me out. Am I supposed to shake it? Or do I do what the other guys do and fist bump? I stare at his outstretched hand for what seems like forever and then finally, I place my own into it and shake.

"Ryan."

"Nice to meet you, Ry."

I shrug, so confused by the entire thing I'm not sure what the proper response is. All I know is that since I started here in kindergarten, this is the first time someone's actually taken a chance and sat down beside me and I'm shocked.

"You don't talk much, huh?"

I start to shake my head, but then think better of it considering what he's just called me out on.

"Not really, no."

"So, Ry. Why do they hate you so much?"

I notice two things when he speaks. The first being the way he shortens my name. I'm not used to that at all. Not even my own mom shortens my name, though to her credit, most of the time she calls me demon spawn so there's no real shortening to be had with *that. What gets me most though is the question he asks. It's a tough one to answer. I could easily tell him why people pick on me so much, but there's this fear that if I do, he'll take off like they did and even though this is new to me, I don't want that happening.*

For once in my life, I don't feel so alone.

"I don't like the same stuff they do, so I guess that makes me a freak."

"Got room in the freak boat for me?"

"You're not a freak. You're just new."

"It's more than being new. I don't know what the hell I did, but whatever it is, it sure makes them rip on me."

"Assholes." We both answer at the same time after a lengthy silence. It's as the word comes out of his mouth the same second as it does my own that it hits me. We're alike, him and I. We're both outcasts.

"I wasn't sure I'd meet someone that wasn't a robot. Glad I did."

What he doesn't realize and I can't admit because I'm still so mystified that this conversation is even happening, is that I've wondered the same thing, and I'm more than a little happy he sat down beside me. I'm not sure I would have done the same if the roles were reversed.

"Yeah, me too."

*****

Jackson was the first real friend I had. He's really the only friend I had. It doesn't matter how much time passes, it stings remembering him so I do my best not to. I never got the chance to tell him, but shortly after the day he came up to me at school, I believed my prayer had been answered. I thought Jackson was Heaven's answer to the crazy amount of prayers I'd been sending them.

At least that was my belief until I lost him two years later.

The thing about Jackson, he was a risk taker. Sure he was nine like me, but he didn't seem to care about things like age, or right and wrong and consequences for stupid actions. He was always looking for ways to test the boundaries, and it being the opposite of the way I'd been living up until that point, I found myself latching on to it. It didn't take long after becoming friends with him for me to change and be the exact same way.

We would take our bikes out and travel trails that were so dangerous, we were never sure if we'd make it back home alive after doing it. We'd bike out of the city and hike until we reached the top of some pretty steep hills and we'd dive off without a care in the world. We'd hide in his shed smoking cigarettes and laughing like we'd just broken the law or something. Man, there wasn't anything crazy enough for us. We seriously tried it all and somehow, didn't end up splattered across the pavement.

It was a miracle.

We were inseparable until just shortly after my eleventh birthday.

The one day I didn't go home with him, was the day everything came crashing down and I lost the only real friend I'd ever known.

He went out biking like normal; while I went home because for whatever reason, this was the day my mom seemed to give a shit and wanted to spend time with me. The thing is, she didn't spend time with me at all. She just had me doing all the shit she'd been ignoring all week. I cooked for her, cleaned the entire house top to bottom and even ran errands. While I was doing all of that, Jackson was out in search of the next death defying stunt.

I didn't find out what happened until the next day at school, but the minute I did, it was like the last shred of humanity I had died. I didn't cry or show any emotion at all. I don't even remember feeling. I was frozen inside, numb all the way through. The other kids acted like they had lost their best friend even though none of them ever gave him the time of day and I sat frozen in place.

The information we were given being a little short on the details of what really happened, I grieved for my friend in a different way. I went in search of answers. If I couldn't bring myself to feel, I figured the least I could do was figure out how this even happened in the first place.

I found out that he biked up to the appropriately named Dead Man's Pass, and in an effort to do what we'd done a couple of times before with no success, he rode off the side, thinking that when he touched down, he'd land like a cat on his bike and just be able to drive off. The thing is, he didn't land on his bike. He separated from it and hit the ground on top of it two seconds later.

He died instantly and the minute he did, I think it was the moment what was left of my humanity died too.

It was when all of this happened that my first real display of anger made itself apparent and just like times before, my eyes changed from their light blue to full black and the kids I didn't freak out with it before, were freaked from that point on.

I hated everyone and everything with such a passion, I didn't think my eyes would ever go back to normal. There was someone I hated more than the kids at school though and looking back, it's where the darkness that became such a huge part of my life later on, began.

I hated God. I hated every single one of the angels. I hated Heaven and everything about it. I started believing my mom was right after all. Anything remotely related to the light was bullshit.

Why give me what I prayed for just to rip it all away a couple of years later?

Nothing about death, especially Jackson's, made sense to me and it bred question after question that I couldn't seem to come up with answers for.

Why take someone that brought so much enjoyment to my life, away from me? What did they gain from giving me something and snatching it away so quickly? Is that really how Heaven operated?

There's this saying that the kids on my block used to repeat whenever someone took something from them and honestly, with what happened to Jackson, it made it true.

Heaven was a bunch of Indian givers. If I knew that this was going to happen to him, I would have said something in my final prayer. As it is now, I regret not doing it because if I'd just thought about it all ahead of time, Jackson still might be here.

I would have told them no takesies-backsies. They weren't allowed to take my only friend from me, leaving me even more alone and miserable than I'd been before I said the stupid prayer to begin with.

It was in that time of complete numbness that I took the final steps to what Lucifer eventually had planned for me, but that at the time I was still not aware of.

I turned my back on the light completely.

Chapter Four
On The Outside Looking In

After Jackson died, things for me went back to the way they'd always been. I wandered the halls alone, still the freak everyone believed me to be. The one thing that was different coming back, was the way some of the girls would look at me. It wasn't a huge difference of course, but sometimes when I'd manage to look up and catch eyes, they were almost always female ones that were there to meet me.

At eleven years old, you would have thought girls would be something that took up a lot of my time, but it never played a part in my life. With the way I was always looked at like a freak, I figured there wouldn't be a girl alive interested in me, especially with the things I could do, and it took too much energy to figure out if there was any truth to it, so I just let it be.

I'd like to say that the looks in the hallway stopped as quickly as they started, but it didn't happen like that. In fact, I think the older I got, growing into my looks the way I did, it got a lot worse. It's another thing about life that I never understood.

Being interested in someone because of the way they're presented physically doesn't make sense. I couldn't wrap my mind around it. If all you've got is the way you look, how do you sustain a life with someone when you're old and everything that once made you beautiful on the outside is sagging, wrinkled and dead?

In my head you don't, which is another reason that dating, sleeping with girls or even hand holding and kissing never even hit my radar. I wanted there to be more than that.

It was also right around then I developed yet another ability I didn't have before.

Mind control.

If it wasn't enough that I could read their minds even when I didn't want to, now I could control them too. By this point I knew what I was, or at least what I thought myself to be. I was more than human and thanks to my mom, I knew it was all my dad's fault. With everything I'd come to learn about him over the years, the worst was that he had no problem using his abilities on the humans, but with each new one that popped up for me, I did the complete opposite.

I had a hard time accepting I could do these things, let alone using them to my advantage. During the years I hung out with Jackson, he became aware pretty quickly of my differences, but never judged me on them. I don't think he understood what the hell was going on and he never brought it up to me, but he also never turned his back either. It was part of the reason I thought he was the answer to my prayers.

Any sane person would have walked away the minute they heard me answer a person they couldn't see, but he didn't.

Too bad the rest of the world couldn't adopt his philosophy. If they did, maybe the changes in me wouldn't have moved quite as quickly and the guy that eventually met Serenity years later could have been saved a life full of horror and things he can never take back.

I wouldn't have become my father.

Being able to control someone, it was a new thing for me. If I embraced it the way my father did, or even the way Lucifer eventually told me to, I probably could have had a whole lot of fun with the people I went to school with, but as it was, after the first time it happened, I wanted to distance myself as far away from it as possible.

Just like every other time a new ability came to light, the day started out like every other one, but unlike the other days, it seemed that just going out of their way to call me a freak and push me around wasn't enough to sustain them. They wanted to kick it up a notch and in the end, got a whole lot more than they bargained for.

*****

"I don't know why the other guys rip on him so much. He seems normal to me."

"You haven't spent time around him. Watch him when he's angry and you'll totally get it."

"Get what?"

"How crazy he is. Trust me, the last thing you want to do is get anywhere near Ryan McGregor."

"He's got really nice eyes."

"Focus, Sarah. He's a freak. Those eyes you think are nice, turn completely black when he's pissed off and sometimes, when he looks at you, it's like he can see right into your head. It's creepy."

These people, they're so freaking stupid that they don't have a clue what whispering is. They're attempting to say all of this without me hearing, but what they don't get is that I hear better than most. I can be at the other end of the damn school and hear what they're saying about me right now.

Carrie is trying to warn Sarah, passing along the facts, but it seems like Sarah is too interested in the way I look to listen much. I just wish they'd shut up already. I don't want to hear any of this.

I have to force myself not to acknowledge them and it's really hard. So when I break and my eyes lift, locking on Sarah's, I can already see that I'm going to pay for it later. Not only does Sarah catch that I'm looking at her and slap Carrie in order to tell her, but now other people are making their way out of class and seeing it too. It also doesn't help that I seem to have stopped walking in order to do it.

"What are you looking at, freak? See something you like?"

Carrie is a bitch, but I don't dare say that to her face. I don't really care if she knows what I think of her, but the last thing I need to do is open my mouth, say the words and get caught doing it. They'd end up calling my mom and she's the last person I want *around here. It's bad enough I have to go home and deal with her every night.*

I don't want her showing up without her pants and underwear. After the shirt incident a few years ago, I wouldn't put it past her to kick it up a notch in the 'embarrassing your kid' department.

"Do you even talk or do you just stare at people?" Carrie snidely asks, and I can already feel my blood starting to boil. Why did they have to make such a big deal of me catching her eye?

"Carrie, stop it. All he did was look at me. It's not a crime."

From what I know about Sarah, she's not like everyone else, but because of the people she hangs out with, I don't trust anything she says. She's probably just like them underneath and I don't want any part of that.

"What do we have here?"

I already knew that we were catching the attention of the other people in the hall, but I hadn't really expected anyone else to get involved, especially since I had no plan to answer Carrie, choosing instead to just start walking again. Apparently, with who just spoke, that wasn't going to happen. Not only did I have to deal with Carrie, but now I had Grant too.

Grant Wilkins. High school jock and all around asshole. Also the guy that happens to be dating the girl I just locked eyes with.

This was definitely not going to end well.

"You checkin' out my girl, McGregor? What did I tell you about that?"

He didn't tell me anything about it, but I'm pretty sure I got the gist of it a long time ago. I wasn't permitted to look at any of them because I was too much of a freak. It worked in my favor before because I didn't want to look at them anyway. To be honest, I still didn't, but one random look was about to change that.

"I wasn't checking her out. I just looked around."

"He's lying, Grant. He looked right at her. He wants her."

Carrie needs to shut her mouth, but after being in the same classes with her for the past five years, I knew that was something that would never happen. She liked making things worse, and the grin on her face proves it.

"Maybe I need to beat some sense into him then."

You need to beat some sense into Carrie.

It was just a thought, but right before my eyes, Grant turned his back to me and faced Carrie. The look on his face, the anger there, it was exactly the same as what he just displayed for me, but now had nothing to do with me at all. It was all on her.

"What are you doing, Grant? The freak that wants your girlfriend is over there."

Someone should smack that smirk off her face.

Again, it was only a thought in my head, but it seemed I wasn't the only one that could hear it. Grant moved in on Carrie and slammed her up against one of the classroom doors. With every movement he made, he was bringing my thoughts to life.

It was scary. The last thing I wanted to happen was for him to hurt her. I might not like the girl, but she didn't deserve to have a guy physically attack her.

You don't want to hurt her, Grant. She's just a bitch.

It's when he turned back around and faced me that I figured out exactly what was going on. He wasn't just reading my thoughts, he was responding to the words. I was controlling him. If I hadn't said what I did, I have no doubt he would have laid into her with his fists.

"Carrie, you need to stay out of this. This is between me and McGregor. You don't have to always be the bitch."

*****

When he called her a bitch, I knew it was my fault. Every move he made was controlled by me and what I had innocently been thinking.

It was weak that day in the hall when I learned I could do it, but the more I focused on it, the stronger it became until if I really wanted to, I could control my teachers and ninety percent of the student body at the same time.

Having these abilities and not being able to put a name to them, or even figure out what it all meant drove me crazy. I was on edge all the time because I never knew what I would make someone do, or what I would hear in their head. It was hard enough walking the halls and being a freak because of what happened to me when I got angry. Add in having to control these new abilities and going to school every day became torture. I hated everything about it.

There was one good thing to come out of it though. Because of what happened in the hallway that day, people went out of their way to remain silent around me. I guess watching Grant come out of a haze the way he did, it put some kind of fear into them. They didn't know for sure that I was behind it, but they suspected, and it made them all take a step back in their harassment.

I was now free to roam the entire school without incident. I'm sure they all still believed me to be the freak, but at least they weren't openly calling me it anymore. When they did see me around, a lot of them booked it out of there quick. I never heard another word spoken about me again.

Three years went by like that. It's only when we graduated from junior high and moved on to high school that the relative peace I had been able to broker came crashing down. The voices were getting worse and my mind was so full of everyone else's thoughts that I wasn't sure which ones were even my own. More than that, something else happened and it would change the course of my entire existence forever.

I was about to come face to face with the devil.

Chapter Five
Time to Meet Your Maker

It's funny thinking back on the time when Lucifer first came to me.

Well, it wasn't the first time he came, but it's the first time I can remember, so to me, in the ways that matter, this was my first dance with the devil.

My life up until that point had been pretty craptastic. After losing Jackson, nothing seemed to matter. I had a new level of hatred for anything remotely human, because deep inside I knew I wasn't. They were beneath me and avoiding anything to do with them was easy. They could have switched things up and embraced me at that point and it wouldn't have changed anything.

If they were human, I hated them on sight.

Looking back now, that was why Lucifer showed up when he did. Reaching that level of pure evil without his guidance, was apparently enough to warrant face time, and he didn't disappoint. It's only when he showed up and started to explain things to me, that I realized he was more than just the devil.

He was the guy that I caught talking to my mother when I was four.

He had a different vessel at this point, so had he not explained things the way he did, I would never have been able to put it together, but I'm glad he told me everything. He might have been the self-proclaimed king of darkness, but his reappearance when I turned fifteen, gave me something to believe in again. Even if the thing I was believing in was the very thing I would come to learn years later I was made to fight against.

It started off like any other day. Wake up, play the avoidance game with Corinne, lose and listen as she told me what a piece of shit I am. Go to school and hear it all over again. Wash, rinse, repeat. That was the story of my life. At least it was until he showed up, looking anything like the fallen angel the world knows him to truly be.

*****

"Can I help you?"

Coming home from school and seeing a random guy sitting on the steps, it's not unheard of. Corinne doesn't exactly shy away from men, but the minute I see him sitting there, his hands brushing repeatedly over his knees, awkwardly, looking like he wants to be anywhere but where he is, I know he's not like the others.

"Yes, you can. As a matter of fact, you are the only one that can help."

Somehow I doubt there's anything I can do to help this guy that he couldn't do on his own, but I'm in serious need of entertainment, so for now, I'll play along.

"What do you need?"

"Am I correct in assuming that you are Ryan McGregor?"

Knowing my name is kinda freaky, but alright, I'm willing to see where this goes.

"Yeah, I'm Ryan. What's it to you?"

"Then yes, my earlier statement stands. You are the only one that can help me."

"You gonna explain that or just sit here and be cryptic?"

"I will give you all the answers you need, but not here. I do believe it would be better for the both of us if we spoke privately."

If he wants private, he ain't gonna get it here. Corinne's got the night shift tonight which means she's home. I could always walk him over to the diner, but somehow I get the feeling he's not gonna fit in there. His suit probably cost more than the place. I'm not sure he'd fit in anywhere around here with the way he looks.

"Well my mom's home, but knowing her, she's passed out. That's about as good as it gets."

"That is where you are wrong. I know it is not the way things are done when two people meet for the first time, but I am asking that you trust me, at least for the next few seconds."

"Some random guy on my doorstep asking me to trust him. That's not weird at all."

"A common reaction, I assure you, but you have nothing to fear from me. I am here for you. It is time that we speak."

Here's the thing. He could be some creepy guy getting his rocks off with a younger dude or he could be someone important and mean every word he's saying. I can stand here debating it, or I can just go with him and see what happens. It's not as if Corinne will miss me if this goes south anyway, so there's really no reason not to.

"Fine. Do whatever you gotta do."

Before I have a chance to react, I feel his arm on mine and suddenly we're no longer standing in front of my house, but in the middle of a park.

"Where are we?" I ask, looking around for some sign that would give away our location, but not finding anything that stands out. "I've never been here."

"That is because until this very moment this place did not exist for you."

"So you just magically conjured up a place for us to talk?"

He laughs and despite how completely off this feels, it's a nice sound. Other than the times I was around Jackson and we laughed together, I haven't had much experience with it.

"Yes, you have had a very tragic existence. That will soon be coming to an end."

"What do you know about my life?"

"I know a fair bit more than your human mind will let you believe. I am aware that you are more than just another human, and I am here because the time has come for you to realize your true place. We will get to that though."

Everything is a riddle with this guy, but there's something about the way he says that I'm something more than human that hooks me in despite it.

"You asked where we are. This, my dear boy is Green Haven. It is the place where everything began."

"Green Haven."

"Yes. It will mean little to you now, but when the time is right it will become everything. For now, just know that you are safe here."

"So why did you bring me here?"

Might as well cut to the chase and get this over with. It's not exactly like I'm looking forward to going home, but I do have shit I need to get done and spending the night in some random place with an even more random person isn't exactly enough of a thrill to pull me away from it.

"I do believe that before I explain that, I must inform you of who it is you are speaking with. Do you not agree?"

Well, I can't argue with that. It would be nice to know who the guy with the power to move me through space is.

"Alright, I'll bite. Who are you?"

"Lucifer."

This is the funniest shit I have ever heard.

"Yeah, okay. So the devil wants to talk to me, huh?"

"I have never appreciated that name. There is nothing devilish about me and the way I am depicted in your texts, as some sort of red demon creature with horns. It is absolutely preposterous."

Shit. I thought at first he was just bat shit crazy and I was gonna have to fight my way out of this, but the way he sounds, how his voice never falters and his eyes, they seem to go dark where minutes ago they had been clear and bright, maybe he's not the one that's crazy after all.

"Deep inside, you know that what I speak is the truth. That I am who I claim to be. Your human mind cannot wrap itself around that truth, but it is there."

"So what if it is. What do you want with me?"

"That is easy. I want you to join me."

"I'm sorry—what?" I ask, choking the words out over the laughter that at any second is threatening to spill out.

"I know you are aware of your differences. Hearing the voices of the dead and being able to communicate with them. Able to tap into another's mind and manipulate it for your own gain. Hearing thoughts. Moving things with the power of your mind. There are more of course, but those are the few you have experienced already. Do you not long to know where that comes from?"

How can he know this much about me? I can buy into his belief that he's the fallen angel, but to know this much about me, there's just no way he could unless he's spent the last few years watching everything happen.

"You are starting to see it now. That pleases me greatly. It means I do not have to explain as much moving forward. I have indeed been watching you, Ryan. I have been keeping watch over you since the day you entered the world."

"Why?" I choke out, still not wanting to believe anything he's got to say, but unable to completely overlook or deny it either. In a strange way, things are finally starting to make sense even if this is one of the most nonsensical situations I've ever been in.

"I first came to you when you were four. I do believe you remember that time in your life, though you have conditioned your mind to forget it. You walked in on a conversation between Corinne and myself. You clung to me then, wanting to be taken from the hell that you had been born into."

The man.

He's the one I thought would take me away. Away from the anger and bitterness and beatings my mom laid on me every night. He hadn't done it though. Just like everyone else he had turned his back and walked away from me.

Why is he coming back now, ten years later?

"I am here now because it is time for me to introduce you to your true destiny. Time for you to realize what it is that you are and work with me for a better tomorrow."

"How am I supposed to do that? I might be different, but I'm still human."

"That is correct. There is much that I need to tell you and I assure you, I will. Today, the intent was to see if you were indeed ready. It appears as though you are."

"Look man, I get it. I've read enough about you, been shown enough to know that you're who you say you are. I mean I don't really know, it just seems to be something I can tell, but if this is gonna work, you gotta start making sense and stop talking in circles. I'm confused."

There it is again. His laughter and that smile. There's no doubt about it now. He's the guy that stood across from my mother and told her the way things were going to be.

He is exactly who he says he is.

"All will be told in due time, son, but for now just know this. You are the first of your kind. The one being in all of creation that is unlike any other. You, Ryan McGregor, are not only human, but a demon. A hybrid. And you will be the one to stand beside me as I end this abomination known as the world once and for all."

*****

It didn't take long after him dropping the bomb of what I really am for everything else to come pouring out. It started first with just who my father was, leading into his disappointment at losing him. It wasn't easy, hearing stories of a man that I never knew, but because of who was telling me, I felt that I needed to listen. If what Lucifer wanted with me was the truth and I believed it to be, then there was nothing he said that I could turn my back on, no matter how hard it was to hear.

Daemon in the end had been a loss for Lucifer, but also one that he got over after learning about me. I was to be what my father couldn't because of his penchant for human women. Where he was strong, I was to be stronger and the very person to help Lucifer bring Heaven and the world as a whole to its knees.

Before any of that could happen, I had to learn about what really lies deep inside me. The best way according to Lucifer to accomplish that meant experiencing the one place I never thought I would have to go because to me, if god and the angels were bullshit and didn't exist, neither could this.

I had to experience where I came from.

Hell.

Chapter Six
The Road to Hell

Ask any fifteen year old guy what they're thinking about and it's pretty easy. Girls, cutting loose and just trying to handle the onslaught of shit your mind and body gets dealt as it goes through the change. The change every adolescent goes through that prepares them for the way life will be as an adult. Now go ahead and ask that of the human demon hybrid guy and watch as his response blows your mind.

Since the day Lucifer walked back into my life after his lengthy absence, I had nothing but time to think, adapt and go through every available motion afforded me as I tried to piece together what I now know to be the truth of my life.

How I have come to exist at all.

Demons; they aren't supposed to be able to procreate. What happened between Daemon and Corinne, was a one off, according to the big man. Lucifer says that to this day he has been unable to figure out how it happened and for him to admit that, given everything he knows and has been through since he fell, is a monumental thing.

Angels have been able to do it for millennia, sleeping with mortal women with the offspring resulting in the Nephilim, but the same was not afforded to those born of darkness. This is where the line for me becomes blurred.

I believe that those beings of darkness were not born, but created. It's the one thing that Lucifer and I do not see eye to eye on even with all the time that's passed.

One only has to look at him to see proof of the way I see things. Lucifer was not always bad. He was a warrior of the light before he fell, which means he was not created bad. It was a choice he made to go against everything he had been taught, exerting his free will, though to get him to admit to any of that is a pointless endeavor.

Before agreeing to bring me to hell, he wanted to make sure I had as much knowledge as possible about me, demons as a whole and even him and the ending he has chosen for himself. With everything he told me, there seemed to be more questions than answers and at certain points I started thinking I'd never get them.

What I do know is simple. This man that years ago told me he would save me from the life I had been stuck in, had stayed true to his word. I had a reason for being, a goal moving forward and once I knew it, nothing could or would deter me from it.

Lucifer breathed life back into me at a time where I was dangerously close to giving up on everything and for that I will always be indebted to him.

The abilities that I have been able to tap into since our first meeting are unbelievable and the ones that were present before, are enhanced with the power he infused me with. Where before his arrival I had been guided by the more human part of me, still able to feel and experience life the way the average human did, now it's the opposite. I do not feel at all. That part of me is cold and I'm running purely on the demonic elements I was born with.

In an effort to bring my true nature to the forefront, there had been trials. Tests he put me through. The first one being to take a demon he had concerns about defecting and bring him to his knees through the power of mind control.

Stepping into a mind, even one as dark and twisted as the being he put me in direct contact with, is a thrill unlike any I had experienced before. It had taken multiple tries to reach inside him, but once there, nothing was off limits. I tapped into the part of him that Lucifer feared had gone soft and with just the right amount of thought implantation, he was back on our side. I twisted the beautiful parts of his mind, reaching deep inside his soul in order to do so, until there was nothing left but charred remains. Completely devoid of the light, which is exactly how Lucifer wanted him to be.

The next test and the one that would guarantee me entrance to what Lucifer deemed my home, was to possess a human. To experience the thrill of breaking one down until they had no excuse but to say yes to allowing me entrance and then doing with them as I wished. An ability I had no experience with, but with my advanced skill with mind control and manipulation, is something I had been able to do with ease.

Roderick Chamberlain was the one to pop my possession cherry. He was not a random choice. He was the only guy in fifteen years that my mom had been with that had the light inside him. Where she'd gravitated toward the darkness with my father and every man after him, she had screwed up with this particular choice and now it was up to me to set it right.

Which is exactly what I did.

One night, about a month after Lucifer first appeared outside my house we were again standing in front of it, only this time, I was going in with a mission. I had to break the man away from my mother long enough to tap into his mind, twist his thoughts and have him give me what I needed.

His acceptance to my possession.

There's a difference between angels and demons when it comes to taking a human vessel. We all require the host's acceptance, but where the angels have to go about things in a specific way, we don't. We can do whatever is necessary to get the result we require, whether that be torturing, twisting or controlling them. Torture at this point in time was something I wasn't ready for, but Lucifer had no issues with me using any other option at my disposal to get the job done.

It had been easier than I thought to pull him away from my mom, meeting him the minute he stepped from the room in search of the bathroom. Placing my hands on his head and entering his mind so easily it was as though I'd done it countless times before. It was only when I ran into the brightly lit wall inside his mind, the one place where beauty and peace dwells that things became more difficult.

Hours upon hours were spent after I had removed him from the house, consisting of me breaking him down, showing him the deaths of countless people he cared about and threatening him through his mind with the same result before he finally caved and said the words I needed to hear.

Yes.

*****

"Now Ryan, you must be ready for what you will experience when you join with him. It will not be a pleasant experience."

He'd been warning me about this since he brought it up and every time I accepted what he had to say, but never really gave much thought past the basic acknowledgement.

As I connected with Roderick, I came to find out just how wrong I was in ignoring it the way I did.

"Is it supposed to feel like I'm being peeled apart piece by piece?" I scream as my body joins with the man now slumped on the ground in front of me.

"Yes. You will experience that in the beginning and then as you completely join as one being, you will begin to feel full."

"Full as in I ate too much or something more?"

"Something far more than that."

He isn't kidding. I can feel it now. Two bodies melding together and not in the way I imagine two people who are in love connecting. There is nothing romantic about this. It hurts.

It feels like someone continuously pouring a drink down my throat so quickly and with so much force that I'm thrashing and choking on it, trying to make it stop, the overfill so heavy it feels like any second I will explode.

It's only when everything begins to even out and I look back toward Lucifer that I see what has taken place. Standing beside him, is my human body, eyes dull and lifeless, completely devoid of everything that made me what I was.

"How is that possible?"

He laughs and I frown. I don't see anything funny about what I asked. Experiencing what I am now is new to me, so he has to expect questions like these until I get a firm grasp on what I truly am.

"How is any of this possible, Ryan? It is the darkness that for years has been trapped inside you just waiting to be freed. The demon. You are guided by it so completely now that when needed, you can separate yourself from your human body in order to fulfill what I need from you."

"What happens to my body while I'm doing this?"

"That's a far simpler question. It merely goes home to rest."

Lucifer smiles before bringing his hands together and right before my eyes, my body vanishes. Seeing it happen, I get to experience just how much power he controls and what that means for me now that I've completed what he requested of me.

"Now that you have been able to possess one of great light such as Roderick, I do believe it's time I bring you home. It is time you experience the true nature of what we are, how we live and what you will become a successor to in the not so distant future."

*****

There is no description of hell in any book, movie or musical endeavor that prepares you for what it really is once you're there. It's that way because unless one of our kind writes of it—which we will never do—it's the same as Heaven in that it can never be truly captured unless experienced.

Getting there had taken a lot of power, something that while mine was strong even at fifteen, wasn't quite on par with the man accompanying me. It had also taken a dark magic spell. One that uses an extraordinary amount of blood, both animal, demon and human, and one that even now I hope to never have to use again as long as I'm permitted to live.

The sacrifices made for that spell alone speak to the level of depravity and pure evil that Lucifer was guided by and my reaction to it at the time spoke to how human I still remained even with my emotional shutdown.

It was and is something that I would never wish on my worst enemy. The spell to open the gates alone is enough to turn someone pure of light twisted.

With the gate open and us having walked through it, faced with the hordes of demons blocking the entranceway, me standing in the very vessel Lucifer had wanted me to possess, it was time for the tests to cease and the learning to begin.

The first lesson being that there are levels to hell, each one more devastating than the last and that's what he takes the time to explain once we've made our entrance and I've come to terms with the sights; smells and sounds around me.

*****

"Ryan, before we enter further into the sanctuary of home, I feel that I should prepare you for the various stages we will be passing through. Seeing as it is your first time here, everything will appear differently through your eyes than my own. I do believe venturing ahead with as much knowledge as possible will serve you greatly."

"Can something happen to me here? Is that why you're warning me?"

"With the power that resides inside you, I do not fear anything happening, but yes, it can if you're not prepared at each stage."

"I don't get it. If I'm a demon like you say, then why can any of this get to me?"

"Because you are walking in with a human vessel. It would be much the same if you appeared here in your own body. You have human blood within you, and it is that blood that will cause the demons that reside here to come for you."

"So you're walking me into a death trap?"

"I suppose that is one way of looking at it. You are under my protection for this visit though, so no harm will come to you. There is one request I have before explaining the various stages."

"Name it."

"I wish to experience what this is like for you. It has been so long since I walked these halls with a being that is not one of the enlightened, and through each stage, I want you to tell me everything you feel. Every sense that you have. Hold nothing back."

"Done."

I've come to learn in my short time with him that when he smiles at me the way he is now, there is a pull to do everything in my power to make it remain there forever. I will stop at nothing to please him because in doing it, I feel as though I'm whole. I'm like that little naïve kid again, doing everything in his power to please his dad.

"Ryan, the way that you think, it amuses me to no end. Comparing yourself to a human is laughable. You are so much more and I cannot wait for you to experience it for yourself. It is why I was so eager to bring you here. I want to share my home with the only other being truly deserving of it."

"You believe me to be deserving even though I'm still learning?"

"Yes, my son. We are always on a path of learning, even one of the fallen such as myself."

There it is again, the smile. The very reason all of this, no matter how overpowering it can be, is happening at all. I am here now because despite how insane and unreal this is, there is no greater sight than seeing this man completely lit up even though we're shrouded in darkness.

"You are my greatest achievement, never forget that."

"I won't, Father."

I've been doing that lately, calling him father. It seems appropriate. The way he is with me, patient and sometimes even kind, he's everything I could ever want in a dad. It's also kind of nice to have someone refer to me as son.

"There are infinite levels to the home I have created here, but in an effort to show you the parts you are most likely to experience, we are to take a shortened route. There will be five levels that you will be shown today."

"What is the one we're witnessing now?"

"The guards. They are some of the most powerful demons that reside here and keep the place safe at all times. There will also be another set of these guards before you reach my chamber."

"Your chamber?"

His laughter fills the darkened hall and where in other times I would be put off with his amusement at my expense, this time I join him.

"I forget that you are still human. My chamber, is what the humans refer to as their bedroom."

"So if these are the guards, what comes next?"

"Lost souls. They are the entities that have not yet reached their full potential and continue to wander. Of all beings here, they are weakest and I often wonder why I keep them around at all."

I've been noticing recently that he reacts this way a lot. He doesn't look kindly on weakness of any kind and apparently that also goes for here at home as well. The callous way he speaks of ridding himself and the world of these beings, whether they're dark or not, speaks to it. I can only hope that I continue to please him as I would hate to become one he looks down on.

"I would never look down on you, Ryan. As I have already said, you are the anomaly. The one being in the world that should not exist, yet does. You command a great deal of power that we have not even tapped into yet and that will serve me well with what happens in the future."

Compliments are hard to take. I'm never sure how to answer, so all I do is bow my head in reverence and nod in understanding so that he's aware I've heard his words. When you live with a mother that from one minute to the next doesn't even care if you're still breathing, hearing anything even remotely kind, is a shock to the system.

It doesn't matter if it's the devil saying the words or not.

"We have the lower level demons next. They are quite a bit stronger than the lost souls, but another entity I have little use for. They serve their purpose and that is all. It is when we reach the next level with the thirst seekers that the real fun begins and where you must be in top form."

"What does that mean?"

"The human blood in you, they will smell it before we even reach them. To them it is the sweetest nectar and they will be relentless in their pursuit of it. You are with me, but any future visits we make either together or apart, you must remember one thing as you pass through."

"And that is?"

"You must bring the demon to the surface. They will still smell the scent of your blood, but it will be overpowered by your true nature. There is much that I need to tell you as it pertains to them, but it can wait until later."

"So what comes after them?"

The grin that spreads across his face, lifting his cheekbones and flowing straight into his eyes tells me that whatever it is, he's pretty damn proud of it.

"My greatest achievement lies beyond the blood seekers, Ryan. It is where the real magic of home takes place."

I'm almost afraid to ask what he means by that. Just because things feel stable with him, doesn't mean that all of this is not freaking me the hell out.

"Ryan, you have nothing to fear. I am aware that all of this is new to you and it will take a period of adjustment to come to terms with what I am telling and now showing you. That is what the next five years are about. It is during that time that you will learn all that I have to teach and take your place by my side."

"You seem so sure of that."

"I am positive because I have seen it. It is the way things are meant to be."

"So," I ask, finally ready to hear what his greatest achievement is. "What comes next?"

"Torture demons. The true beasts of the place humans deem as hell."

Now that I've heard the types of demons I'm going to encounter as I make my way through, there's only one question *that remains unanswered and even though he's said not to fear anything, I can't help but be afraid that his answer is going to be even worse then everything he has already said.*

"Which one am I?"

"Why, Ryan my boy, you are combination of all of them."

*****

When he told me I was combination of both the best and worst that hell had to offer, it didn't seem real. It was some kind of joke. As dark as my thoughts have gone over the years, they have never once reached the point of torture, but as I was soon going to learn, what I'd already been through hadn't been anything at all.

The worst was still to come.

Chapter Seven
Bleed For Me

My first experience with Hell was also the first time I learned about my ability to block Lucifer out. At the time, I had no idea I was even doing it, believing that it only worked on the demons, but I picked up pretty quickly with the way he had gone from hearing my every thought to hearing nothing at all that I could do it with him too.

If he knew what I really thought about his home in the beginning, I'm not sure what he would have done with it. It wasn't that I hated everything about it, but it was overwhelming. It got better over time. My visits there afterward weren't nearly as bad, but that first time, the minute we made our way through the hordes of demons that occupy the space, I wanted to turn around and run home again.

What I had with Corinne was practically angelic compared to what I faced with Lucifer there.

It started with the smell. It was so powerful that I wished that I had my senses stripped completely. I didn't want to smell something so putrid that it made me puke. But puke I did and when it happened, where I expected him to laugh, he just nodded as if he'd been expecting it. I just don't think he expected it to happen the fifteen times that it did the entire way through.

By the time we made our way through to the blood seekers, I was drained completely. I wanted to sleep and by sleep I mean, die for a week just so I could repair the damage that being sick caused. What started with the smell of old garbage and decaying flesh, turned into me wanting to cut my nose and eyes out because it cut so deeply through both senses.

Blood, despite what people would make you believe, does have a scent, but the sight of it is even more dangerous, especially with the quantity strewn throughout the halls of Lucifer's home.

When he mentioned torture in the beginning, I went in expecting it, but my expectations were not what I was met with. He didn't just torture people there, he massacred them and despite my uncaring and unfeeling persona, I felt it.

I felt every bit of it as though it was happening to me.

It was that visit that made me begin to doubt my alliance with him. Being human, even if there's nothing but darkness underneath it, means that I can't ever do what he wants me to, at least not all the way.

I can push away the emotion, pretend they don't exist, becoming as cold and unfeeling as he is, at least to the naked eye, but it won't ever be gone. I will crack, the same way I did during our visit and it will happen at a time that will eventually lead to my end. I just know it.

It's the human way after all. He's right about that.

Humans are weak and I was proving it just in the way I felt the need to hide everything away from him. I believed that if he saw that side of me, he wouldn't want me anymore and I would have been right back where I started and it was something I couldn't let happen. Being with him still would have been better than anything I would have gotten in my old life.

He would rescue me from the life with Corinne, the pain and misery that came along with it and show me a better way. A way that I can adapt to and become stronger because of.

It was around that time that I became conflicted. What I knew I wanted and what I needed, were slamming into each other and at any given time, I didn't know what side would ultimately win out.

How could a fallen angel like Lucifer be considered so wrong when the way he was with me at the time spoke to an extreme level of caring and concern and ultimately what I imagine the love of a father to a child to be? If that's what Heaven perceived to be wrong, it was easy to see why he'd been removed. The magnitude of Lucifer when he allows people to see the real him, can't be contained, so he had been sent down and created a place where it could be on his own terms.

This ability I had to block him, I decided to put it away. I couldn't use it with him again. For weeks he had been a father to me, someone I could look to for advice, guidance and who was determined to show me the right way. The rest of creation may not see it the same way, believing the world to be something far more worthy than it is, but I knew his vision of the future was true.

What he wanted to do, it *was* the right way.

All of that doubt, learning that I could block him and what I truly believed was the right way and his part in it, brought me to the next lesson that he had to teach me.

In order to truly embrace all that he was ready to offer me, I first needed to come to terms with the demon lying dormant inside. I needed to become one with the darkness and in order to do that, I have to become one with the blood.

*****

Watching the group of drunken women as they converse on the park bench, I feel torn. Lucifer has explained that if I hoped to survive and prosper when I finally took my place at his side, I first had to become one with the blood, but it didn't make it feel any less sickening.

The idea of drinking someone's blood in order to placate the demon made the very human part of me sick to my stomach.

It's wrong.

"Tell me what you are experiencing."

"Is it customary to be able to hear their hearts beating when you tune out the rest of the noise around you?"

"Yes. When you are finally able to free your mind of the chaos that the world creates, you are able to tap into the more primal part of what you are. The bloodlust. Hearing their heartbeat, it is the first step."

"And the second?"

"Your throat will become dry, you will ache with a need so strong, you are unable to contain it and the only way in which to cease the agony your body experiences will be to feed."

"Feed how? I mean I get the gist. I'm going to drink the blood, but how do I go about doing that?"

"Every demon handles it in a different way. Some prefer to feed right from the vein, which is where the vampire concept was created, while others choose to stab their victims first, and focusing their power on the wound, drain the blood into a goblet or other available drinking device."

"Which way do you prefer?"

"Ryan, there is nothing more pleasurable to me than experiencing the human in every way imaginable while I drink of them."

Does he mean what I think he means? Is drinking blood some sort of sexual experience for him? I'm a guy and I've got urges all the time, so I get it, but I can't see that being something I can get into. Being with someone that way, it can't just be primal and violent. It has to mean something more.

"I must admit, I never thought you would be the romantic sort."

"So you do look at this in a sexual way."

"I do believe the word you used earlier is more accurate."

"What?"

"It is a primal and violent experience for me, but if you must know, yes. When I partake of human blood, feed the hunger that lies within me, I find it extremely satisfying in a sexual way."

"If I'm different, is that okay?"

"Of course. As I said, each entity handles this particular experience in a different way. You seem to be more reserved in your thinking, though I should warn you, the romantic notion you have about the way anything related to sex should be, that will be wiped out rather quickly. It is nothing but a fable."

If drinking blood is a part of who I am, I'm okay with that, but this is something I can't be okay with. I know he believes me to be blinded with the way I think about sex, but it's not human at all.

It's just me. I will never use drinking blood in the way he does. Whenever, if ever I'm with someone, it will be because I have finally allowed myself to be completely in love with them.

I will accept nothing less.

"You will never experience love, Ryan. It is not in the cards for us. We have been damned to the darkness for a reason. Love is something afforded to those who belong to the light."

"Are you telling me that you never experienced love before you were cast out?"

"The only love I have ever known was that of a son for a father. The true art of love, that is present in soul-mates or that of the beloved, it was never afforded me. Love has no place in the darkness."

Here comes the conflict again. I don't want to believe him. I want there to be something more despite knowing deep down there isn't and he's right. I want to believe that if it can happen so easily for the humans, then it has to happen just as easily for someone like me too. Even for Lucifer. We cannot be damned to this life of darkness and not experience something as simple as love.

"Love is not simple, Ryan. Your way of thinking just proves how naïve you are to the truth. All one needs to do is pay attention to the way humans are so fickle in matters of the heart to see how right everything I have told you is. Real love is messy and it will leave you more broken than anything you will ever experience with me."

I have nothing I can say in response so I just nod my head in acceptance of his words. It does no good to question him and as he's already proven on more than one occasion, he is nothing if not completely honest with me at all times. He does not twist things in order to keep me in line. He shows me the full picture, no matter how cruel it may be.

"Are you ready?"

"Can one ever be ready for something like this?"

"No, I do not believe they can be, but Ryan, once you experience this, things will drastically change. Everything that seems so wrong now will begin to make sense."

"Is that how it happened with you?"

"My experience greatly differs from yours because I am the one that created all that you are about to experience. What happened with me can never be repeated again."

"Will you ever tell me what you went through?"

"One day, but until then, I do believe it is best we stay in the here and now. In this moment, there are three delicious smelling women that I do believe require our attention."

*****

All conversation ceased at that point and I accepted that it would be all I would get from him until he deemed me worthy enough to tell me more. We made our way over to the three women and just like Lucifer said, it changed everything forever.

*****

Getting her away from her friends had been a lot easier than I expected it to be. With all the stories on the news about women being abducted, stolen by strangers in the middle of the day instead of the night the way most assumed, I figured that separating them would be difficult.

I meant what I said to Lucifer. I didn't want to use this experience as a chance to satisfy primal desires. This was about accepting the life I'd been born into, coming into my position by his side and nothing more. It was a means to an end.

Unfortunately, the girl named Erin seemed to have other plans as she slipped her body into mine and attempted to force herself on me.

It seemed unreal that a girl would be the pushy one, but that's how it happened and once her body connected itself to mine, I wanted nothing more than to shove her away. I don't do well with touch and especially from someone like her. A girl who only likes what she sees on the outside and decides that she's going to have it, whatever the cost. That's the worst kind of touch there is.

"I saw you looking at me. You and your friend. I was hoping you were going to make a move."

This girl has no idea that what we just did is not a move. It might be for the man that was now leading the other two girls away in an effort to enjoy his feast on them, but it wasn't for me. She has something I need and that's it, but it's not something I can just open my mouth and tell her. I've got to take her away from this public setting and then I can finally let her see the truth.

"I would have been over sooner if my friend didn't want to fight with me over you."

I've learned from the best, so the smirk I give her, the one that's laced with innuendo, has the desired effect. Her eyes go from bright to clouded over with the desire she's experiencing. It's not my first experience with a female reacting to the way I look, but with as uncomfortable as it makes me, first lying to her and then having her react to the lie, you would think it was. There isn't anything about this experience I enjoy.

"I'm glad you won. My apartment's just around the bend there. What do you think about taking this inside?" She points across the street and down an alleyway and in that moment I see clearly the way this is going to go.

We're not going to make it to her apartment. I'm going to get her alone in the alley, push her up against a garbage can or the wall, anything really, making her think I want her and then I'm going to drain her of every last drop of blood she has pumping to her over eager heart.

This must be what he was talking about. The overwhelming need to feed on her blood. It's so strong that my head is pounding, my heart is pumping hard and fast and I'm having trouble breathing. It takes all of my restraint not to take her right where we stand. Focusing as much as possible, I nod slowly in response, taking her hand in mine and picking up speed until we're crossing the street and the alley is only steps away.

""Let me grab my keys, they're in here somewhere." She says, her voice breathless as she comes to a complete stop and starts fiddling with her jacket pockets.

"Why wait? No one's around and I've got a thing for public places. Tell me you want me as badly as I do you."

The physical pain that talking this way causes me, I've got nothing to compare it to. I have never been so completely turned inside out in my life. Leading her on this way is wrong, but the willpower I would need to stop it before it starts is dulled by the smell of her blood pumping in her veins. Sliding my hand over my jeans, feeling the small blade there, I swallow down how wrong it feels and let the desire for a taste of her wash over me.

I can see why Lucifer believes it to be sexual now because the sensations that rise, they are similar to what I can only imagine sex would be like with someone. I've been turned on before, I am a guy after all, but taming it is easier for me than others. I have no desire whatsoever to do anything with anyone, so as quickly as it comes it fades. At least that's how it was until now.

I will not do it. I will not do as Lucifer has done before me.

Pushing her against the wall and crashing my lips down onto her neck, purposely staying away from her lips, not wanting this meal to be the first experience I have with kissing, I slide the blade quickly from my pocket and as I pull away I see the hunger for me laced in her eyes. As they take me in, I smile and this time it's genuine. This smile is for what is about to happen, which is not at all what Erin believes it to be.

Raising my hand, I see as her eyes take sight of the blade and within seconds, all desire is gone and it's replaced by the one thing that does turn me on. Fear.

She's scared of me. She knows what the reality is now and as she struggles against my arm, which is now draped tightly across her neck, keeping her frozen in position, I reach into her mind.

Erin struggling will not make this experience euphoric and I need it to be. I need to experience this the same way others before me have and I will settle for nothing less.

"We've discussed this, Erin. You said you wanted me to put the blade to your throat. That it would turn you on. You want me to be your first time."

Her body goes lax in my arms as the mind control and thought implantation has the desired effect and I bring the blade to her throat, pushing it deeper against her flesh. It's in that moment that I experience it.

The skin has broken open and the blood that I could feel just in the few seconds we spent together is now rising to the surface, the smell intoxicating. No longer able to control the urge inside of me to taste, breaking my rule about making this sexual, I bring my lips back to the spot I just sliced and I slide my tongue first along the small line of blood that's risen and then place my lips fully down and begin to suck.

It is only as her body goes limp from the blood loss a few minutes later that I realize what I've done and back away from her, watching as she slumps down on the ground like a paper doll. The way she looks passed out in front of me is not enough. The taste of her is flowing through my veins now, her vitality, the very beat of her heart now becoming one with mine and making the hunger even greater.

I want more with her. I cannot let it end this way. Slowly bending down until I am kneeling before her, I tip her head up with my hands and really look at her. Placing a tender kiss to her cheek, I place my hands around her neck and content with the way they're positioned, I close my eyes and twist until I hear the sickening snap as her lead lops to the side.

Watching in awe as I release my hold on her, she falls to the ground and it's in that moment that I have everything I need. Now I can feed the way Lucifer wants me to without fear of this becoming something more.

Slicing the blade across her throat and moving down to her wrists, placing identical cuts on both, I begin to feed, first at her neck and then down until I have had as much blood as I can stand.

Hearing footsteps behind me as I continue to suck on her wrist, I smile through the blood that is now dribbling down my face as I turn and face the intruder to my good time.

"I assume it was everything I said it would be?"

"It was everything, Father. The only question I have now is—when do we do it again?"

*****

Up until that point, I had deluded myself into believing that the things I was doing, what Lucifer was teaching me wasn't bad. It's almost as if I was in my kitchen again, four years old and believing everything to just be an elaborate magic trick.

What I did to Erin, even now years later I can never go back and undo or completely forget about. There may not have been anything romantic between us but in a lot of ways, she was my first and feeding from her before snapping her neck and ultimate killing her, completed the transition.

Had I not taken her blood that day, I'm sure it would have happened with someone else, but I might have been able to hold out a little longer before it did and maybe even spare their lives, something I will never be able to do for Erin.

No matter where I go from here on out, how bad things became after, her blood still runs through me as clearly as it did that day and no amount of running, living a better life and trying to do the right thing can change it.

When I killed Erin, I truly became a monster.

Chapter Eight
Thrill of the Kill

After Erin, everything became frenzied. The hunger continued to grow until denying it became impossible and a year after that first time with her and what I experienced in the alley, I laid to waste 2,875 humans.

I want to say I was specific with my victims, only choosing those with the purest blood, but the hunger made it so that any specification I might have had was quickly thrown out.

I fed on humans whose blood was so riddled with drugs it was often amazing they were still alive. I drained victim after victim that suffered from a myriad of diseases and I didn't think twice about it. The blood was delicious and I devoured every drop.

There is an ecstasy that occurs when feasting on pure blood though, and it was that particular type I gained an addiction to. It had gotten so bad that after a time, Lucifer had to put me through his own version of detox in an effort to break me of it. But even after withdrawing for months, I still ended up going back, and every drop, pumping through my veins to this day still brings me pleasure that I hate admitting to.

Virgins, whether male or female, those that were untainted both by the world and sexually were a delicacy that Lucifer let me in on rather quickly after the incident with Erin. It was those types I sought out, leaving their families broken as I made sure that when I was done with them their bodies would be found. I don't know if it was my penance for what I had done to them, wanting their bodies found so they could be buried in the right way or not, but whatever the reason, I did it and not one human body went undiscovered.

The murder rate spiked, and it was so bad that at one point a vague description of me made it onto the news, but never once were they able to snap a picture or put forth anything more than speculation.

Despite what the papers and news would have you believe, I was smarter than other killers. I was faster and better at what I did. Let them attempt to figure out why the bodies were drained of almost every drop of blood inside them. They would be wasting their time and I could continue doing what I did unnoticed.

It was and still is my dirty little secret.

After a year of putting me through my paces, draining victims, possessing them, it was now time for me to head back to Hell, this time in my own body. It was during this particular visit that I came face to face with my past and no amount of running now will ever get me away from it.

It's the one thing that I have never brought up since it happened and remembering it now in such graphic detail, is a sickening reminder of just how dark I became during my time with the fallen angel. It was a time I want nothing more than to escape from, making it someone else's tale and not my own.

Being a demon hybrid, one that lacked everything needed to make me one with the other humans I was surrounded with at school, should have burned the twisted feeling of guilt that I felt inside seconds after it happened, but it doesn't.

This is the one secret I can never let slip, because it's the moment in time where my allegiance to Lucifer became absolute. It had been happening in baby steps up until that point, but this, it crossed me over.

I was finally worse than the devil himself.

*****

"Another test? When are you going to admit that I'm exceeding your expectations?"

"You know, there was a time where I had my doubts about you," he says, as if this answers my question. "It appears as though

you have embraced the demonic quite easily. Along with the ego that comes with it."

Grinning, having yet again earned his approval, I continue to push. "That does not answer my question, Father."

"You are well aware you have exceeded all expectations, but that does not mean you are free to roam on your own just yet. There is one more trial that we must see to before I can be assured you are ready for what will come in the future."

"I already did the whole 'making my way through hell' thing though."

"Not in the manner at which you will be in a few minutes."

"How is this different then the time before?"

Now it is his turn to grin and though I should feel frightened by it, I'm not. Where things were too much to handle in the past, now I find myself craving whatever path he wishes to guide me down as I know it will be a perfect fit for me. I will gladly accept this next test and pass it as I have all the others.

"You will walk through the stages of hell alone for this test. It is how you adapt as you enter the domain with the other blood seekers that will give me the answers I need."

"Is this where you tell me you're concerned I won't make it out alive?"

"I have no such concern. After spending the last year and a half with you, teaching you everything I know. Watching as you embrace the demon inside you, concern is the last word I would use as it pertains to you."

"What word would you use?"

"That is a question for another time, Ryan. Right now I want to see how quickly you annihilate that which I have placed before you."

"You want to see me fight?"

"I want to see you reign supreme in the fight, yes. It will bring me an immeasurable amount of joy."

Anything that brings this man joy, I am willing to be a part of. There is no grander sight then to see him smiling, his hands clasped together in the ultimate display of glee as he watches his greatest achievement take form.

"I get the feeling there's more going on. That there is something you aren't telling me."

"You would not be wrong in your assumption, but this is a good thing. There is a surprise waiting once you have completed this particular trial and I cannot wait to see your reaction as you come upon it. Wanting your reaction to be natural, I am afraid that is all I can say."

"Is this a reward for a job that will be well done?"

"In a manner of speaking, yes. Ryan, this is your final test. Once you have done as I need you to do and you experience what comes at the end, we can move forward to the ultimate goal."

"The thing you still haven't told me about?"

"That very thing, but as I have already said, there is a reason for me not sharing it with you quite yet. I need to be sure you are ready for what needs to be done and will be most willing to help me achieve it. A place that a year ago you had not yet reached."

"But I am going to when I finish today?"

He nods and as is the usual between us, I know this is where his sharing ends and everything that comes next, I will have to learn on my own.

"Go forth, Ryan and try not to enjoy the massacre too much."

*****

He had given me a tidbit of information during my last visit, knowledge that I had to use as I defeated the lower demons, wanderers and everything that would bring me to what awaited with the blood seekers. The minute I rounded the bend and picked up on their blood, his words from the past had risen, guiding me forward with what I needed to do.

"You must always remember that until the day of mastery comes, you must remain in your demon form in order to make it *through. It is my hope that as you grow and become one with the evil inside you that you will enjoy it as much as I."*

Having mastered how to bring the demon up until it was the one in control, it was easy to transition from what I had been when I entered, to the demon that walked into the lion's den.

As expected, the seekers could smell the human blood that tainted my flesh, but they would not get the opportunity to taste it. The only one lucky enough to taste blood that day would be me, and taste blood I did.

I made quick work of them, making them all surrender before partaking of their blood. Having tasted more than my share of tainted blood when I'm topside, the tangy taste of the demons didn't faze me, each passing demon that I enjoyed just pushing me forward in my pursuit.

I had to get to my reward at the end, no matter the cost. Even if I had to obliterate every last demon placed here to serve.

It's only when I reached the end, mere steps away from the torture chambers that I saw it. Came face to face with my reward and it was the very last thing I had been expecting to find.

It wasn't even a reward, but another task and this one, even more important than the others before it.

*****

"I always knew there was something off about you, man."

The voice. I know it. It's one I haven't heard in six years and also one I never expected I would ever hear again, but here it is now, loud and clear in my mind, almost as if it's real.

"How is this possible?"

"You're standing here, same as I am. Why don't you tell me?"

"I know how it's possible, but the real question is, how are you here? How is this where you ended up?"

"Live fast, die young and leave behind one hell of a good looking corpse, my friend. How could you believe I would end up anywhere else? I mean, have you met me?"

Jackson.

This isn't a mirage or dream. He's real. It wasn't in my head. It's his very real voice standing in front of me, looking worn, yet more alive than before.

My childhood friend, the answer to my prayers, actually here. In hell.

"This isn't what I wanted. You deserve better than this."

"Says the guy that just drank the blood of twenty bloodsuckers."

Is it possible that what I held onto so tightly, believing it to be my secret alone, was never that way and Jackson is aware of what I really am, or is he just finding out now?

It doesn't take very long for him to let me know.

"You're one of us. I think I knew it when we were topside, but now I definitely know for sure."

"Yes, but you're human."

"Not anymore."

"What does that mean?"

"You know what it means, Ry. All you have to do is open your mind to it. You know what happens next."

He's right. I do know what this is. The pot of gold at the end of my rainbow, the thing I would earn when I made it through successfully, is not a reward at all. It's not something to be treasured.

It's another trial and one I'm not sure I am able to face. For all the darkness I have embraced, the memory of Jackson, is the only thing that still remained completely bathed in the light.

"Now you see what you must do, my son."

No. No fucking way am I doing this. He can put me into the chambers and force my hand that way, but I will not do what I know he wants me to now.

I will not kill Jackson.

"You can't ask this of me, Lucifer." *I spit out, erasing the image of him as a father from my brain entirely and keeping it impersonal by calling him by his given name.*

"I am not asking anything of you. I know what lies deep inside you. Even now as you stand here looking at the first person you ever allowed close, you feel it too. You cannot run from that. You need to embrace it. It is what will deliver you where you need to be."

I want to fight against everything he's saying, but he's right. I am angry. Angrier than I've ever been seeing Jackson here. He never should have ended up here. He was a good person to me during our time together. The best person. I'm angry with myself because I know I'm the reason he's here now. It wasn't the way he died or the things he did in life that did it.

It was me.

Just as much as I'm angry with myself, I'm angry with Jackson. He should have fought harder, and not left me. Not when I believed him to be the answer to my prayers for all those years. Screw him and his selfishness, getting himself taken before he should have been.

He deserves to die.

"Do it, Ryan. Let that anger guide you. The hate you feel toward him, use it to end his very existence. The moment you do, you will be free to be what you were always meant to be."

"What's that? Your protégé?" I snap as all of the blood rushes to my head, making it almost impossible to see. I am so livid at the situation, at the fallen angel and the demon standing on opposite sides of me that I'm losing the ability to think altogether, let alone logically.

"No. That is what you are now. What you are meant to be is far greater. You are going to be the very thing to end the world."

This is excruciating. Him talking so easily about ending the world, it should feel wrong. Deep inside, the human part of me is screaming at me to back away from all of this because it's not right, but I can't because the pleasure I feel, hearing of the world being brought to its knees, is infinitely stronger.

I need to see the world end. I want to be right there watching it as it burns to the ground. I want to feed on every single one of the useless pathetic humans, throwing them away like garbage when I'm done with them and then rejoicing with the only person that has ever given a damn about me.

Lucifer.

"You must do it now, Ryan. If you wish to achieve all that your mind is conjuring, then you must do what is needed."

Yes. I have to do this. He's right. Jackson is a reward after all, because he is going to be the sacrifice I give to my father to prove I am ready.

Focusing my attention back on my old friend, I no longer see the boy I knew, but the demon he has become. Every day spent with him as a young child is erased and all I can see is the pain and agony left behind. The very things I must use now to end him.

In a weak attempt to fight against me as I appear behind him, using my power to move through time quicker than he can keep up with, I finger the blade that has appeared in my hand, covered in the blood of countless victims I have spent the last year devouring, and as he turns to block me, I slide the blade up and around until I feel it pierce his flesh.

The blood appears, but not as it would have appeared during our time together as children. This time appearing in total darkness, devoid of all color, black as the night itself. The scent of it, more intoxicating than any victim before him.

"Finish him off."

Heeding the words I hear clearly in my mind, I pull the blade only to plunge it deeper inside him of him a second time, repeating the motion ten more times before backing away completely and surveying the damage done. It's only when I see his dead and vacant eyes staring up at me that I lose control and let the hunger and rage take over completely.

It's in that moment that I level with him my final blow, one that will assure he never comes back again, killing both the human that is buried somewhere deep inside as well as the demon that has just enticed me into his web. I slice his throat, so deep across that it severs his neck from his body completely, his head crashing to the ground before his body falls from my hold seconds later.

It's been done. The transformation is complete.

"Well done, Ryan. Now we can truly begin."
"Begin what?"
"The end."

*****

I wanted to feel remorse for what I did to the one person that cared enough about me to give me the time of day, but after everything was over and we had left to go topside again, nothing would come. I couldn't feel anything, least of all remorse. At least in terms of negative emotions or ones that humans normally feel when something like this happens.

There was one thing I did feel though.

Pleasure.

There was a moment before I stabbed him that I felt this perverse sense of pleasure over what was to come and it was impossible to turn away from both in the moment and after it. Ending Jackson, bringing myself even closer to the only father I have ever known, it pleased me to no end.

I wasn't the only one who felt that way. A lot of things were a blur for a long time after that, but I remember Lucifer going all out when it was over. He arranged to have a group of high ranking demons join us to have a celebration. The first one I'd ever experienced at that point. It was then I realized that there was still so much for me to learn.

The way demons are depicted in books, art and especially in movies, up until that point I had assumed were all wrong. In meeting with some of the higher ranking beings that reside in hell, I realize they aren't as far off the mark as I thought.

Where my only experience has been dealing with demons that looked like the humans they possessed and killed, wearing them around like meat suits both at home and during their time topside, I got to see that there are more than one type. There are ones that do have horns and other facial deformities that set them apart from all that I have seen and know. It is these ones that stay hidden, only making their presence known when Lucifer calls for them.

Times of celebration rank pretty high in them making an appearance and it was during this celebration that I finally met them, as Lucifer laid out to them exactly who I am and what my role will be when the time comes. It is there we gorge on humans, drinking their blood in small intervals, in an effort to keep them alive for the duration of the party, and where their darkest desires are manifested and brought to life.

It's in watching them all at their most primal and sated that I realized how different I am, and it had nothing to do with being human. I realized my way of thinking, though guided by darkness, is still somehow trapped within the light.

The realization was something that I didn't want to acknowledge and was something that I blocked Lucifer from being able to see because of the consequences, but it is definitely something that I personally could no longer deny.

I couldn't do what those demons had done with the human women and men that were in our company. I had no trouble partaking of the wine that is their blood as my hunger would not allow me to ignore it fully. It's everything else. The rape, the beating, the pure violence that takes place all in the name of celebration, where I was at my most displaced.

It's because I realized how easily that could have been me. With the human blood that runs through me, I could have easily been one of their victims and witnessing what they do to those they perceive as a treat, I wanted no part of it.

Possessing a human, running around in their skin, turning their lives upside down for fun, even now years later I can understand because I'd spent that last year and a half enjoying doing that. I can even understand feeding on them, using them in that way because in order for beings like me to thrive and continue on, we need it the way a human needs to eat and drink and breathe air. Everything else though, it reminds me of my mother and Daemon and I found myself turning my back on it.

I want to be better than Daemon. I did then and I do now. I was determined in that moment, in the middle of a celebration over what I had done to Jackson, to be better than my demonic father. Smarter.

In the end I wanted to be the one left standing because I knew deep down I was better than all of them and no matter how long it takes, I was determined in that moment to prove it to him.

Lucifer would see that the way he had been doing things wasn't working and we would work together to make it better, or I would go to my grave trying.

Jackson's death had to mean more than a reason to have a sick celebration.

It would mean the rise of the darkness and the end of the world, just the way Lucifer said, but with one big difference.

It would happen on my terms.

Chapter Nine
You Can't Go Home Again

The last thing I expected after everything Lucifer put me through was for him to tell me I had to go home again.

By home, I don't mean Hell, where I could remain for eternity and be happy. No, he meant my *actual* home, with the mother that couldn't stand me, the neighborhood kids that hated my guts and the place that I never truly fit in.

The *last* place I wanted to be.

It's where I end up though and no amount of arguing with Lucifer changed it. This is what he wanted and if I wanted to please him—which at the time I did— I had to go along with it or risk losing everything.

He wouldn't have taken me out of existence. He needed me too much to do that, but he would walk away from me for a time. Having had no one to count on until the day he showed up on my doorstep, him walking away was the last thing I wanted to happen.

A year and half before, I had been given this gift. Someone out there in the world said I was important. That I had a purpose and they cared about me.

If I hadn't given up on having my prayer answered at that point, I could have easily believed Lucifer coming and taking me under his wing the way he did, was the answer to those prayers. He had given me something from the moment he stood in front of my house that first day that could never be replicated.

He gave me a family and in a twisted way, he had given me love. The one thing he said I would never experience.

It's those things that made his decision hard to stomach. After being taken under his wing and shown how to exist with the power, then being told that for the next few years I had to go it alone, it felt like it was all being ripped away from me.

Again I was being left behind.

I would never be good enough for anyone.

The emptiness I felt that day, still twists me up inside. For every second I spent saying that I didn't want to feel, I sure as hell felt a lot that day and none of it was good. It was all twisted and crazy and drenched in loss.

Lucifer had become my father. He was the only being in existence that I trusted enough to let in. The one that understood the way I am, pushing me to be even better, and I wanted to hold onto that forever. You never want to lose the purity that comes along with the love between child and parent and I expected him to feel the same.

I have no doubt that he felt something, but he definitely didn't feel things the way I did. He may have looked at me like a son, but to admit to something more beyond that, would never happen. The ease at which he delivered the blow of me going home proves it. A father who loved me unconditionally wouldn't have done it. Which meant only one thing.

Lucifer didn't care.

*****

"Ryan, come. Sit with me. There is something I wish to speak to you about."

I do as he says easily, sitting with him, looking out at the world around us and seeing everything much the way I did when we were in hell. It's dark here even though we're surrounded by nothing but the sunlight. The perfect atmosphere for delivering bad news.

"What do you want to talk about?"

"The time has come, Ryan. It is time for me to go home so that I may begin putting everything together for the undertaking."

"When do we leave?" I ask eagerly. If we are going to be putting together the plan that will inevitably end the world, I can't wait to start.

"That is what we must discuss. There can be no 'we' in this equation. It is something I must do alone. Which means until such time as I need you, you must return to your life."

"My life is here with you."

"It will be, but not quite yet."

No. See. I don't want him to do this. Not when things are just starting to make sense. Where I feel more comfortable with everything we've been through and I'm desperately aching to serve him in a greater way. He can't just walk away and end it.

"Ryan, I am ending nothing. We are just going to be separated for a short time."

"Why do we have to be separated at all?"

"In order for things to go according to plan, we all have to play a role, and right now, as much as it pains me to say it, there is nothing you can do. I have to take care of things from here on out."

"Why come to me at all if you were just planning on leaving me in the end! You're no better than Daemon and Corinne."

"I do not appreciate your tone."

"Well I don't appreciate being used, kept in the dark about this supposed undertaking, and then ditched because you don't need me anymore."

"Have you not heard a word I have said? You will still play your part and you will do it well, of that I have no doubt, but right now there is nothing you can do. Just I as promised as a child, I will return to you."

"Everybody leaves. That's easy. It's the coming back that's hard and you know what I know? Most people when they leave, take the easy way out and stay gone. You're going to do the same."

"Have I not stayed true to my word every time it has come into question?"

"Yes, you have, but that doesn't mean shit."

"That is where you are wrong, Ryan. If I can remain true to my word for as long as we have been together, then you can be assured that I will continue to do so. This is not me using you and walking away. This is me planning for a better tomorrow."

"My tomorrow is going to suck."

"As I have said before, Corinne's time is coming. She will pay for what she has put you through for all of these years, but only after the undertaking has come to pass. She will be the first that I make burn."

Here he goes again, promising me things the way he's been doing from the start, but all they are now are empty words. I don't believe he'll come back no matter how many times and ways he tries to make me see differently.

Lucifer's leaving me, the same way everyone else has..

"You will see. When everything has been put together, all possible outcomes outlined and handled, I will return and together we will see your destiny through to its end."

Pulling me to him so that all I'm able to experience is the closeness between the two of us, I allow myself the brief enjoyment that comes from the embrace. It's the first time I've been embraced this way. How fitting that it's taking place mere seconds before he expects me to go back to my ordinary existence while he leaves for god knows how long.

I want to hate everything about this moment, but I can't. He has calmed the beating of my heart until it's nothing but a dull hum in my chest and warmed me where before I had let my anger over the finality of the decision turn me rigid and cold. I would do as he said because of the way I feel for him, but I wouldn't like it or agree.

"I understand how you are feeling, Ryan. Everything you feel in this moment is right. I wish that things could be different, but I am afraid they cannot. What I must do now, everything I must put together, I need to be sure you are protected from so that we can see this through to the end. I cannot risk anything happening to you."

"So now you want me to believe you're doing this for my own protection? What is it really, Lucifer? Do you want me with you, but want to protect me? Or do you just want to say whatever is necessary to get rid of me for good?"

"I cannot believe you would even think the latter is a possibility after what we have been through, but I will repeat *myself again so that this time you are able to hear me clearly. I wish to protect my greatest asset. My gift. You. I wish to keep you safe because of what you will mean, not only to the world, but to me in the future."*

"Fine. I get it now. Go. Do whatever needs to be done. I won't hold my breath on you returning."

*****

Adjusting back, even though we spent most of our time topside was harder than I thought it would be. The only thing that was easy about the time I spent apart from him, which ended up being close to three years, was avoiding my mom.

If she had been going out of her way to avoid me before Lucifer came calling, she was even more determined after I got back. It was like she knew what was going on the minute I showed up, though it took several months after to bring it up. It was the one and only time we spoke after my return. Life with her was still hell for those three years, but there was a lot more fear on her end now that she knew the truth of where I'd been.

The only glimpse of the woman I'd known before came when she learned about Roderick. She hadn't taken that well and the true evil inside her, the very thing that made her the monster she was, it came out as she learned the truth about everything. Reacting the way she did, I was prepared for whatever she would level me with, but just as quickly as she reacted to the news of Roderick, she backed down.

It was almost as though she believed that anything done against me would earn a visit from Lucifer, which was something I'd come to learn after the fact, she definitely didn't want happening.

*****

"So you're alive after all."

"Gee Corinne, don't let the concern pour out all at once." I answer sarcastically as I head through the front door and right for the stairs that will lead me to the only real sanctuary I know.

With as much as she pays attention, I'm surprised it took her this long to talk to me. I would have thought she would want to get this out of the way when I came back weeks ago. Doing it now seems pointless. What's happened that suddenly warranted attention from her now?

"You're different."

"Thanks for taking time out of your busy schedule to notice."

I really don't wanna be having this conversation. I want things to be the way they've been since Lucifer tossed me back here. I want to continue going through the motions, marking each day off the calendar until he returns. I want my mother to continue ignoring me. It's the only thing that makes this situation remotely bearable.

"He's come back hasn't he?"

"Who?"

"Lucifer."

"What do you know about him?"

"I know a lot more than you think I do, boy. The only reason for you being this confident has to do with him and I don't like it. It's not smart for you to be spending any time with that man, Ryan."

"Why's that, Mom?" I ask, rolling the unfamiliar name off my tongue. She might be my mother, but I've gone this long without calling her by the name reserved for people that actually give a shit about their kids, I've got no problem continuing. "Could it be because he might actually tell me the truth? Something you haven't done in the last seventeen years?"

"This is a truth you don't need to know!"

"Who decides that? You? Just because you were stupid enough to screw a demon and get knocked up doesn't mean you get to dictate what's good for me. You lost the right to that a long time ago."

"He's filling your head with garbage!"

"Yeah, I know. Telling me the truth about what happened between you and Daemon, what he really is and what I am, that's all garbage. Cut the act, Corinne. The 'good mother' routine isn't working."

"This has nothing to do with parenting. This is warning you about what you're getting yourself into."

"Why would you do that? Because you want me to believe you care? Newsflash, Mom. You're too little, too late."

"You can sit there and act like a little cocky little prick all you want, but I know a hell of a lot more about that man then you do. I know what he's all about and maybe if you would just open your eyes, you might learn a thing or two."

"I don't need your kind of learning. So what if Lucifer came? What does it matter to you? Are you jealous because for once there isn't a demon here trying to get in your pants?"

"Watch your mouth."

I've had enough of this conversation. We're just gonna keep going around in circles. If she isn't beating on me, starving me or generally treating me like shit, she's not bringing anything to the table. I want to bail out and I know just the way to do it. I know something she doesn't.

"Whatever happened to Roderick?"

"What does he have to do with this?"

Damn, she catches on quick. Oh well. It's time she knows the truth. What happened to him after I was done with him. What her twisted little boy did. She needs to know all of it. In graphic detail.

"Didn't you ever wonder why he didn't come back? Why after he screwed the shit out of you, he just went poof?"

"What did you do?" she asks, her voice shaking as the reality of what I'm saying takes hold. Call it all the time I spent in Hell harnessing the power I control, but I want to see just how far I can twist her. I want to see this sick bitch break right in front of me.

"Who said I did anything?"

"I can tell by the look in your eye. The sick and twisted happiness there. The evil. You did something. Oh Ryan, what have you gotten yourself into?"

"You really wanna know, Corinne?"

She walks toward the sofa and nods her head as she sits. Typical reaction. I've seen it many times over the last two years when I would visit the families of my victims and watch them react to the loss of their loved ones. As if sitting down is gonna ease the pain of what I did.

Nothing can do that.

"I possessed him at first, rode around in his skin for weeks. When Lucifer brought me to hell the first time, to the very place my 'father' lived with him, I let the demons have their way while I stood inside enjoying every minute of it."

"No! You didn't do that. You're not like Daemon."

"I am exactly like Daemon, Mom. I was created from him after all. That's why I look so different from you, because I'm more demon then human. It's also why you hate me so much."

"I don't hate you."

"Lies. Beautiful little fairy-tales you tell yourself to feel better, but nothing but wretched lies. You hate everything about me, every part, even though I'm more like you than you want to let on."

"So, you let demons feed on him? That's all?"

This is where things get interesting. I'm sure she wants me to say that's all I did, but it's not. I had a special kind of fun with Roderick, something that I haven't had with another human since and it's about time she knows it. She needs to hear just how sick and twisted her son really is. Maybe then she'll start understanding what all of her bullshit the last seventeen years has caused.

"No, that's not all."

"What else?"

"When I finished with him, I brought him back here while you were working. If you want to know the rest, I think you're gonna have to come with me."

She'll come because in her own sick way, she loved Roderick and needs to know everything that happened in order to come to terms with it. She's completely human and for me to get the most impact from this, to really break her the way I want, showing her *the aftermath of what happened that night has to be the way I handle it.*

She stands and heads toward the stairs and as she silently begins taking them two at a time, more than a little eager to get this over with, I follow behind her, the entire time pleased with what's about to happen. I've made sure to stay out of this room since I've been back and she didn't have a reason to be, which means the carnage, it will all still be there.

The minute she pushes my bedroom door open, I hear the gasp and watch in amusement as she falls to the floor, the impact of what she's seeing overriding every sense inside her.

There's blood covering the walls around my bed, and the bedspread, the one that had been white with blue lines down the middle, is now completely brown in shade, the blood staining it and lasting the duration of my time away. There is even a hint of the iron like smell coating the entire room so there can be no doubt about what happened here.

It's this moment, where she's at her breaking point that I tell her everything, leaving no detail hidden.

"Do you see the claw marks in the headboard? That's where he tried to free himself from everything I did to him. He was no match for me, though. He was trapped, unable to free himself and after a while he gave himself up to it."

"All of this blood, it's his?"

"Yes. It's all his. After making sure he was securely fastened and unable to break free, I took this blade," I say, pulling it from my pocket and shoving it in her face. "And I began slowly peeling back the layers of his flesh, watching as the blood spirted out, hitting the walls, eventually slowing and draining into the sheets and mattress instead. Once the first layer had been completely peeled, I began on the second, and the third, each one giving more blood than the last. It was then that I enjoyed drinking it, even going so far as to lick it directly off the sheets in order to get the full effect. His screams only added to the intoxication of the moment. It was amazing."

"He—was—a good—man..." she chokes out before her voice fades off completely.

"A good man that got involved with a woman that wasn't so good. He met the end he was supposed to."

"Why? Why do that to him? Did you do this because he was with me? Is this some sort of revenge for the shit I put you through?"

"No. It was a lesson. It was a way to pay homage to the only real father I've ever known. Lucifer did not want me to go as far as I did, but by the time it was over and he saw what I had done, he was nothing but pleased. So was I. I've never felt pleasure the way I did when I drained the very life from the man you fancied yourself in love with."

"You sick son of a bitch. Get the fuck out of this house! I don't want you here."

She's hitting me now, her weak little punches having no impact. I'm stronger than her now. What worked when I was little won't anymore. I can make Roderick's fate her own in a matter of seconds, but I won't because Lucifer said he wanted to be the one to deal with her.

"Watch your language, Corinne. I don't think I like your tone. As for me leaving, I'm not going anywhere."

The minute her teeth make contact with the skin on my arm, biting as hard as she can manage, I wrap my free hand around her throat and pulling her away, tossing her across the room until she falls heavily on the floor, cradling her head the minute her body makes impact with the wall.

"This is the way things are going to go. You're gonna go back to ignoring me and pretending that I don't exist, all the while making sure that you never forget that I do exist. Who I am, what I am, you're never gonna forget because if you do, I'll find a way to make you remember."

"Screw you. If you want me dead so badly, just do it. Got nothing left to live for anyway."

"I want to do nothing more than end your pathetic existence, but that's not my decision to make. Your time is coming and when it happens, just remember that more than anyone else, I will enjoy it most of all."

"You're evil…" she spits out, her voice weak, the pain finally taking hold, bringing me a sense of joy like none I've experienced before. It's about damn time she found out what all her torture feels like.

"Tell me something I don't know."

Walking back to the door, I begin to walk through it, turning one final time as I make my way through.

"As always, great conversation. Now do us both a favor. Clean yourself up, go to work and screw another few assholes like the whore you are."

She winces, whether from the physical pain or the emotional impact of my words and all I do is smile. It all makes sense now. Why Lucifer came to me and why I had to come back. It was all for this moment right here. The moment that I showed my mother just who held all the control.

"And Corinne, this isn't over."

*****

After that, I came and went as I pleased, though I still managed to stick to the way things were before I left. I went to school, did what I had to do there, putting up with the bullshit from the other kids, all the while plotting ways I would make them all pay when the time was right.

What happened with Corinne that day changed me even more. Where I had been able to separate from the things I'd done while allowing the demon to have complete control, I could no longer do. I experienced it all, both human and demonic.

I was alive again and for the next three years, while I waited impatiently for Lucifer to make his return, I did everything in my power to enjoy every minute of that living.

The first way to do that? Possessing another human. Bringing what happened with Roderick back to the surface and reliving it through another poor idiots eyes.

Only this time I didn't just torture the person, I utterly destroyed him in every way imaginable.

Chapter Ten
Feed the Beast

The more I repeated the same routine, the more the restlessness grew. I was a few short months away from graduation when it finally became more than I could handle.

I'd been doing my best to control my urges since coming back, and for a while it seemed like I had a good handle on it. As hard as it was to pass these ants in the hall and resist the sweet scent of their blood, I somehow did it and managed to detox completely.

He didn't tell me that I couldn't continue with the bloodletting, but I felt that if I wanted to secure his return, I needed to do things a certain way. I was determined to change the way things were being run, both in Hell and here, and in order to do that, I had to change too. Into something that while still dark and dangerous, was better.

Grant Wilkins couldn't let me do that. No, he had to get in my face again, only this time it wasn't about the girl it was when we were in middle school. This time it was over the very girl I'd made him slam up against the lockers. His new girlfriend.

Carrie.

It seems she'd only gotten worse in my time away. She was more vindictive than ever and with what happened that day in the hall years ago, she was gunning for one person in particular.

Me.

She wouldn't face me herself, so Grant had been the one to reach out to me first and this time, I didn't cower and back down the way I did then. I was stronger now, and there was no way I was going to let him get the better of me. As hard as I had been trying to fight my urges, they all came to a head that day and it's something that despite knowing all I do now, I will never get the chance to go back and fix.

What happened with my mother, was what pushed me forward as he slammed me up against the locker and attempted to put the fear of god into me.

It's only when he backed away, content that he'd scared the shit out of me enough to screw off and go back to whatever it is he does when he's not picking on people that the plan formed in my mind. Once I had it all worked out, all that was needed next was the right time and by the end of the day, I found it.

*****

With practice done for day, I watch as he makes his way off the field and just as he reaches his car, attempting to pull the keys from his pocket, I grab him. With a combination of my newly focused strength and the power, bring him to the ground until he passes out.

Sliding the keys from his hands, I toss him in the front seat, slamming the door, looking around me to make sure I don't have an audience before sliding in the backseat myself and preparing for the next step. I wasn't just gonna shed my own body and possess this one. No, this time I was gonna do something far worse.

Once we joined, I put the key in the ignition, my final destination clear in my mind.

Carrie's house.

If the bitch was going to attempt to bring me down by using back doors instead of facing me herself, I was going to make her pay in the worst possible way.

Reaching her place and meeting her at the door, shoving away her attempts at trying to kiss me, I push my way into the house and let the fun begin.

"I thought you were never gonna get here."

"Sorry babe, practice ran late, but I'm here now. We alone?"

"The whole house to ourselves." She confirms and I grin. Yes this is going to be easier than I thought.

Teenage girls never cease to amaze me. You would think their parents would smarten them up, but it seems that the older I get, the easier they become. They'll give it up to anything with a pulse.

"I want you. So choose. Kitchen. Right here on the floor, or your room."

I want her to choose her room because if someone does decide to come home early, it would take less effort on my part to make things appear to be another way. The less power I have to use in this, the better, since I'm pretty sure what I'm trying to do now isn't something Lucifer will think highly of.

We're selfish beings, but there's a time and place for it and doing this the way I am, I'm risking exposure and that will make him angry.

"Bedroom." She says and I can barely contain my pleasure.

Taking her by the hand, I lead her up the stairs, relying on Grant's own mind to guide me and once there and inside with the door slammed behind us, I push her down on the bed and climb on top of her, making it appear as though I'm about to give into the temptation of having her underneath me, but really just wanting to keep her body still for what comes next.

"Babe, do you trust me?"

"Yes." She whispers before leaning up into me and crashing her lips down onto his. I refuse to believe that it's me she's kissing because there's no way in hell I would be with her this way in my own body. So I let the object of her affection enjoy a few moments of pleasure as I plan out what comes next.

"I want to tie you up. Do you have a scarf or something I can use?"

My voice—his voice, it's husky now, what she's doing to his body having the desired effect, and when she nods and points to her closet, I slip off the bed, immediately grabbing two before making my way back over to her.

"Slide up on the bed."

She does as I ask, but what she doesn't seem to realize is that I don't want to tie her to the bedpost this time the way I did with

Roderick. No, this is going to be quicker than all of that. I don't want to torture her. I just want her gone.

Stretching her arm up, I take a hold of it, but before she can react to the fact that I'm not tying it up the way she thinks, I stretch the scarf between both of my hands and wrap it around her neck, pulling on the ends until her legs start to thrash in an attempt to escape.

"Hush now, ugly girl. I'm giving you what you've had coming for years."

She thrashes more as I tighten the hold around her neck and before I know it, I see her skin changing colors, going from a darker red before all the air is cut off from her body and it begins to even out, turning more pale. It's only when her body goes completely limp and leans against where I'm positioned behind her on the bed that I finish what I started.

I take her neck between my hands and I turn it until I hear the snap. The same sound that Jackson made during my time in Hell, Carrie does now and the rush of satisfaction that rushes through me, knowing that this bitch is finished brings the darkness even more to the surface.

Now the real fun can begin.

Carrie's parents, they're due home within the next half hour and after recognizing in the past how long what I want to do next will take, I know they will enter just as I've finished what needs to be done. Grant, as much as I want to torture him the way I have with others in the past, has something far more entertaining in store.

He won't die the way his useless girlfriend did, but he will pay.

Pushing the power forward, I use it to control him, pushing him to move from the spot on the bed until he is directly on top of her again. From there I make him lean into her neck and as he sinks his teeth into it, I make sure every ounce of strength I can bring to the surface runs free so that he's able to break through and open her skin up. The minute the blood breaks free, the scent of it setting every nerve ending in me on fire, I make him drink.

Minute after minute passes as he devours her, pulling back every few minutes in order to be sure that her blood, the very blood I'm making him eagerly consume is not only flowing down his throat, but is evident on his lips, his clothing, even going so far as to have it pool in parts in his hair.

It's only when she's drained completely that I've done what I set out to do. As I make him walk from the room, the sound of a door unlocking greets me and it's in those few seconds before it opens completely that I finish what I came here to start. I pull myself completely away from Grant, giving him full control of his body back before again using the power to hide myself from view.

Carrie's mother walks through the door first and as her eyes scan the staircase, she locks straight on the blood drenched boy and the scream I hear her make turns my insides out.

But not because it's wrong. What happened to Carrie and what will now happen to Grant, couldn't have been more right. It turns me inside out because the level of pleasure and satisfaction flowing through me is so strong.

This is exactly what needed to be done and as the woman rushes for the stairs, pushing past the now confused and stumbling Grant, who has gotten a full view of his body now covered in blood, I hear her scream again as she comes across the deceased body of her daughter.

*****

It was sick and twisted, but the pleasure I experienced that day was impossible to reign in. It knew no boundaries. Taking those two bullies, those worthless, piece of shit humans and treating them the way I did, it was fun for me and even with all the time that's passed since it happened, it remains one of the only good memories I have of that time in my life.

Who knew possession and desecration could be so fulfilling?

Chapter Eleven
He Is Always Watching

The change that I thought I could bring to Lucifer and the one that would change the way everything in Hell had been run, faded shortly after what happened with Carrie and Grant. It was like what I did and the brash way I did it, it turned something around inside me. I became more reckless after that. I made mistakes, throwing caution to the wind and it's a miracle I didn't end up caught or worse.

The response that I wanted from Lucifer came, but not from him. He sent one of his trusted minions to warn me about my behavior. It was my first taste of being called an abomination by the man I considered a father and in the years since it happened, it stuck around. Where Lucifer had told me numerous times before that what I am meant something, I was coming to find out that what I meant wasn't good at all.

I was the mistake in his design. I should have never existed. I knew it deep down, but the point was really being driven home with the bodies that I laid to waste. I started out with a reason for every kill I did. I would drain bodies because of the urge for blood. I did away with Carrie and made Grant end up in jail for her murder because I wanted payback. The others though, I was killing for killings sake.

It's only when I met her that everything started changing again.

Ava Greavey.

When I finally moved out of the house, putting distance between Corinne and myself, allowing her to finally sleep with both eyes closed again, I didn't know where I would end up.

I didn't think it all the way through, but with the wealth I'd been accumulating from underground poker games I would use the power inside me to win, I had more than enough money to get a place of my own.

This is where I thought I was smart. I was hiding all of this from Lucifer now, taking the warning I'd been given and running with it. If he didn't agree with what I'd been doing and I wanted him to come back the way he promised he would, I had to do things in secret. I was still screwing up and doing things recklessly, but this time, no one was any the wiser. Not the humans and definitely not anyone in Lucifer's camp.

I got hooked up with underground poker games when I first got back to town. When I wasn't home scaring the shit out of my mom, or at school pretending to be something I'm never going to be again, I was there taking their money. After establishing a good losing streak, even allowing myself to be on the receiving end of more than a few fights that left me bruised and broken, I used the power to my advantage and started winning.

I never lost after that.

I would hop from location to location, staying under the radar with my wins until I racked up more than enough money to move out. In the end, I settled for squatting in an abandoned building and that's when I met Ava. Apparently I wasn't the only one at the time that was hard up for a place to be or not sure where I belonged.

For the first few weeks after she showed up, I did everything in my power to get rid of her. The last thing I wanted was someone there with me, least of all a female, and I made sure she knew it. I hated anything to do with women. They were useless. They either wanted me because of the way I looked or for what I could give them, and none of that appealed to me.

Even though I backed down on my decision to change things, I still couldn't bring myself to be like Daemon or even like Lucifer. I didn't sleep with them. I didn't even touch them.

The thing about Ava was, she was different than the other girls I'd come across over the last few years. She was possibly more broken than I was and by the end of our time together, by the time the whole truth came out, I wanted to touch her.

*****

"Ryan, do you think you'll ever tell me where you go at night?"

"Why does it matter? I just go out. You can't stay inside all the time."

"I don't believe that. You come home, if you can call this hellhole a home, and you're wired. Fidgety. It's like where everyone else is settling, you're not. Are you out doing drugs or something? Is that why you won't talk about it? I mean if that's it, you gotta know by now I won't judge you."

God, she talks a lot.

I've spent the last six months living here with her, doing all that I can to get her to leave. I purposely went out and got into a fight, coming home slashed up and practically broken, hoping that seeing me that way would scare her away, but it didn't. All it did was make her more determined and more of a pain in my ass.

"Are you ever gonna leave me the fuck alone?"

"Nope. Sorry to disappoint."

It's not exactly a disappointment anymore, even if I hate admitting that. With her not leaving, I've gotten used to having her around. I don't want her gone as badly as I did before.

"I could tell you where I go and what I do, but you wouldn't believe me."

"Try me. There's not much I don't believe in. This world is screwed up."

She does this a lot, going out of her way to tell me how much of a mess everything is. First it was her life, then it was her family and now it's just the entire fucking world that's batshit crazy. It's another reason I'm starting to handle having her around.

It's because she's right.

"You really think I'm out doing drugs?"

"Come on. You know how you are most nights. Are you gonna sit here and tell me that it doesn't make you look like a drug addict?"

She's got a point. I suppose in a way with what I'm doing every night, I am an addict. The worst kind too because no matter how long I've managed to go without before, I can't do it now. I'm a slave to the blood. To the gratification I get when I kill someone. Feel their life drain right before my eyes.

"Doing drugs would actually be a lot better than what I do."

"I followed you once, you know." She says and this actually scares me. If she followed me on a night where I let the anger and the blood lust control me then there's no telling what she'll do with it. She'll be able to ruin me.

"Learn anything in your stalking attempt?" I shoot back, attempting to deflect from the rise of fear I feel with a good shot of indifference.

"Yeah actually, I did. I learned that you think poker is worse than drugs."

The relief I feel at hearing she's only seen me going into poker games is tremendous. This means that my secret, who and what I really am, is still safe.

"For some people it is."

"So you are an addict."

"Something like that. Why does it matter?"

"Honestly, I don't know. I just think that since we're pretty much shacking up together, we're kind of all we have, ya know? I wanna be sure you're alright."

This is what sets her apart from me. The way she can just freely admit that she cares for me. That even though I did my best at keeping her at arm's length, she's still managed to connect to a small part of me and considers me all she has in the world. I don't want to be that. Not for her and not for anyone.

I'm nothing.

"I do more than play poker, Ava."

"What do you mean? Are you like in a gang or something? Is that why you look so sick right now? Are you gonna have to break my kneecaps?"

For the first time since this conversation started, I laugh, finally broken of whatever this is I'm experiencing. I need the *laughter. It will make what I'm about to say easier. She might think that I'm all she has, but she's about to find out that she's alone in that just like she is in life.*

"Kind of. I hurt people. Torture them," I pause giving her a chance to react before continuing with the worst part. "For fun."

She's gonna get up, grab her stuff, which isn't a whole lot and she's gonna get the hell out of here. It's the only thing left that I can use to make it happen and be sure she stays safe.

It has to happen because I swear if she stays any longer than she already has, I wouldn't be able to control myself anymore. Ava will make me feel and with what's coming, feeling is something I can't afford.

She doesn't leave, though. She sits there still as a statue and then after a few seconds she smiles, and it's a smile that I've seen reflected on only one other persons face in the last nineteen years.

Lucifer.

"It's about damn time. I was starting to think you were gonna hold onto that forever!"

*****

Ava wasn't the innocent human girl I thought she was.

She was something far more sinister yet beautiful at the same time. I didn't learn it right away. I spent a lot of time falling under what I now know is her spell and being completely oblivious to the truth of her origin that was lurking just under the surface.

It was only after another few months together that the truth came out and when it did it was the last thing I expected to hear.

Ava, well the original human girl, had died a year before in a hit and run. Lucifer had taken control of the body at the time, keeping it under lock and key until a worthy enough demon would inhabit it. The visit I received from his henchman about my behavior, was a smoke screen so that he could put the real weapon in play.

She was the weapon and as time wore on, she became my weakness. Spending the time that I did with her, even taking her out with me at night towards the end, it was giving Lucifer his control of me back even though he was nowhere near ready to come topside. As long as I was spending time with Ava more than I was alone, things were moving along the way he needed them to.

My reckless ways became a thing of the past and I began controlling my urges again. By the time he was ready to make his presence known, I was so controlled you would almost question if I had a demon inside me at all. I was the master of illusion because the urges were still there, strong and crippling as always, but with her help, I managed to keep them under lock and key so that no one knew they existed.

The struggle during that time came from the lack of control I had as it pertained to her. She was beautiful to me right from the first day she stepped into the abandoned building, but it was something I never acted on.

There was only one instance where the control I'd managed to build began to crack, and it's the one moment now, looking back, where I realize that I felt long before I ended up in Stephenville with my assigned task.

Ava, for all of the darkness surrounding her, was preparing me for what was going to take place in the future even though I didn't know it at the time. It's because of the time spent and our growing closeness that I was able to use my own free will in what would come later. I'm sure of it.

She asked me to take her dancing one night. Her reasoning had been that it had been years since she had experienced what it felt like to truly be locked into someone's embrace as they led her around the dance floor and it was that one moment where my resistance to all things female began to thaw.

We went dancing and I held her in my arms and while nothing about it felt right because all I was filled with at the time was an ache I couldn't begin to describe, the human part of me was attracted to her. It was dancing and holding her that close, breathing in her scent that I experienced what real attraction felt like and found out that maybe it wasn't something unheard of for us after all.

*****

"You know, I am starting to think you don't like me much."
"That's not true."
"If you grip me any tighter, I'm thinking you might actually break me. Is this your first time dancing with a girl or something?"

Am I really that transparent? I thought with the way I moved around the dance floor with ease that it would appear as though I knew what I was doing, but it's obvious that I'm failing at it, just like I always do when it comes to anything remotely human.

"Is it that obvious?"

"Yeah, sorry. Just relax okay?" she says and the smooth way it comes out as she rubs her hands across my shoulder drives my heart rate up even more. Where I felt cool a second ago, the heat in my body has also risen, making it hard to think, let alone continue to move around with her this close.

"With the way you look, I would've sworn you had done a lot more than this before, but shit. I really think you're clueless. How far have you gone with a girl?"

"I'm not discussing that with you."

"You're a virgin, aren't you?"

"None of your business." I snap, definitely not wanting to get into this. With my reaction to her alone, it makes it impossible to even form the words, let alone speak them aloud. I also don't want to admit how badly I want to change that status with the way she feels pressed up against me.

"It became my business the minute I felt this." She grins at me before sliding one of her hands down to where my very visible reaction to her is now completely on display. I feel my cheeks grow hot and hear her laughter seconds later.

"Give in to what you want, Ryan. You're twenty for fuck sakes. You can't live like a monk forever."

"That's where you're wrong."

"What makes you so much better than me or anyone else that chooses to be guided by what their body wants?"

"I don't think I'm better, Ava. I just know the way I want things to be and not even dancing here with you like this and how it feels will change it."

"What is it that you want?"

"I want to be with the person I love."

"And if I said that I love you?"

"My answer would still be the same because it's not real. I'm not worthy of love. It's not something that's afforded to someone like me. You know it to be true because you have seen the things that I do when no one else is around."

"That's what makes me love you."

"You might be right, but it's not what makes me love you. I'm sorry, Ava, but I can't do this with you."

*****

The moment I felt what I did with her, is the moment Lucifer made his comeback, bringing with him not only the truth about who and what she really was, but also the knowledge that my time had come and the undertaking was now about to begin.

It was officially time for my part in the ending of the world to start.

Chapter Twelve
Date with Destiny

I always expected that if he showed up again, there would be more fanfare involved.

Lucifer making his way topside after a three year absence should have meant something. Appearing and going about business as usual didn't seem like a good enough move for him, yet that's exactly what he did.

It was just like the first time, only this time around, he didn't have the option of sitting on my front step waiting for me to show up. No, this time he was lounging out on the craptastic mattress I'd bought and dragged into my makeshift apartment with Ava.

True to his word he came back, and this time, armed with information. All that I would need moving forward with the plan he had elaborately put together, only that wasn't all he brought with him. He also brought the truth about the girl that was standing beside me the second we walked in.

The human girl that wasn't supposed to have any knowledge of him or what his plans were, was getting a full view of him and he didn't seem to be bothered by it in the slightest.

I suppose that should have been my first clue that there was more going on with Ava than I knew, but at this point, I had been so shoveled full of shit, I didn't know what end was up. I was just going through the robotic motions.

*****

"You're here."

"Did I not tell you that there would be a time when I would return?"

"Yeah, you did. I'm guessing that time is now."

"It is. There is much we need to discuss."

I turn toward Ava, prepared to tell her whatever I have to in order to get her out of here. I definitely don't think she wants to hear whatever it is Lucifer's gonna have to say. She might have been alright hearing I'm a killer, but knowing I'm a demon and in league with Lucifer on top of it? I have serious doubts she signed up for that.

When I turn though, she's looking not at me, but at him and she's smiling. Looking back at him, he's wearing the same smile, the twisted one that they share together and that's when it hits me.

They know each other.

"I am sorry for the deception, Ryan, but what you are starting to see, is indeed true. We do know one another."

"How?"

"Ava is a member of my army. She is loyal to what we are trying to achieve."

"She's a demon?"

"Yes."

"And you're choosing now to tell me that?" Before he can answer, I'm spinning around, turning my outrage on the other person in the room that deserves it. "Why didn't you just tell me that months ago?"

"She did not tell you because I would not allow her to. Though she did want to."

If that's supposed to make me feel better, it's not working. Nothing about this feels good. Not only has this girl that I thought was fully human been lying to me for almost a year, but Lucifer put it all in motion. The man I chose to trust years ago is turning it around on me making me wonder why I did it at all.

"It had to be done."

"No, it didn't! I've already been through every imaginable test you threw my way and passed them all with flying colors. I've been loyal to you for years. You didn't have to do this."

"Yes, I did. I know you do not see it that way, but this was my final test before I could appear again. I needed a great deal of time to pass in order to make sure you were ready."

"What test?"

"I needed to test your humanity. Ava is quite beautiful and with as sympathetic as she was to you and everything she had learned about you, I had to know if you would give into her."

"Well did you get what you needed?"

"Yes. You are much better than your father. The humans do not tempt you in any way. You had a moment where I thought maybe you would break, but you easily caught yourself."

"You manipulated me."

"I am sure it appears that way. It was not my intent to do that, but it is what it is, as they say. It needed to happen and this is the best way possible."

"As long as you enjoyed the show."

"It would serve you better to disregard the hostility, Ryan. As I have said, I needed to test you. I have done it and I am pleased with the result. We can now move ahead even stronger than before."

"And where does Ava fit into that?"

He turns to her and all traces of the smile he once wore is gone. He's all business now as he regards her, first with a nod and then with a flick of his hand.

"She doesn't fit into what happens next. She has served her purpose well, so now she will go home where she belongs until such time as I need her again."

"You're gonna fill me in on everything now, right?" I ask as Ava takes her leave and disappears, going back home the way Lucifer intended, or at least that's what I assume she did. With everything I've just learned though, he could have annihilated her and I wouldn't know the difference.

"I am, but first can I just say, what I witnessed from you as it pertains to this girl, the ways in which you changed, yet didn't break were absolutely outstanding! You have succeeded where your father before you has failed me."

I'm not sure I wanna admit it, but with as close as I came to giving into her the night we danced together, I think maybe he should have continued testing my resolve. If he needs to be sure my *humanity won't come through on this mission, I have to think the line I almost crossed may cause issues.*

"You have been tested enough. There will be no more. Even if you had given into Ava the way I was attempting to make you, she is a demon so it would not have been frowned upon. She is one of the most sexually charged I have in my arsenal. If anyone can break someone, she can."

"Was any of it real?"

"She genuinely cared for you, Ryan. None of that was fabricated. She cares for you just as I do. It is not the pure way that I am sure you imagined it to be, but we are capable of caring for someone, especially someone as dark as ourselves."

It should have made me feel better to hear that, but it didn't. The only thing I remotely enjoyed hearing was that Ava was designed to tempt someone. It meant that the way I was attracted to her, the gravitation I had in certain times was all normal and expected. I hadn't been going against my normal hatred of women at all. I was feeding into the illusion that only she could create.

"That is one thing about you that concerns me."

"What's that, Father?"

"The first time you experienced the blood, I assumed that you would be like your father or even a little like myself, but you were not like either of us. The blood did not turn you the way it does with most."

"You did say we all have different reactions. Maybe I'm just the anomaly or abomination you believe me to be."

"It is true that you were not to exist and in that regard it makes you an abomination, but you are also much more than that. Please do not let my opinion sway you from the rightful place you will take."

"Which you're gonna tell me all about now, right?" *I ask, more than a little eager to get on with it. Anything that can erase the stench of betrayal I feel right now would be welcomed with open arms. I don't want to think of the ways I feel as though he let me down anymore or I might not be able to see this through the way he needs me to.*

"Yes, Ryan. I do believe it's time for you to learn what your role will be in the falling of all that live in the light."

*****

There's something funny about the word destiny when it's said or pertains to me.

When I hear the word, I think of something that is based in the light, but with Lucifer standing with me, telling me what my destiny is and exactly what I will mean in the grand scheme of things, there was nothing pure or beautiful about it.

I was to aide him in the falling of Heaven and Earth. They would both crumble under the weight of what he has planned and even though my role seemed small in the beginning, in the larger picture it couldn't work out any better for me if I wrote it myself.

I would take a rightful spot by his side, working beside him until such time as he was ready to hand the reins over.

It means that at some point in the future, I was slated to become the devil himself. Before that could happen though, I first had to deal with a human and it was one he couldn't resist showing me once he let the proverbial cat out of the bag.

As we prepared to take sight of her for the first time, he informed me that she would be the one to become his bride. The perfect specimen to have by his side as he brings Heaven to its knees.

*****

"The brunette that you see crossing the grass and heading toward the building, the one with the wave in her hair and perfectly sculpted curves with legs that seem to go on for miles. She is the one."

I don't see anything all that spectacular about the girl he's pointing out, but I'm not about to admit that to him. We're witnessing her from a significant distance even with our heightened eyesight, so there is a chance I'm just not seeing the entire package. She is as plain as they come from where I stand, and with what he has told me about what I'm expected to do in regards to her, I see it working out easily.

The entire time we've watched her she has been alone, which tells me she's the same as I am when it comes to keeping away from others. It will either make it easy to get close to her or that much harder, but with the way I look, I'm sure it will be the former. There hasn't been a girl that can resist my charms yet, and I'll take pleasure bringing this one to her rightful place.

"She wields a great deal of power, a lot of which she has not yet harnessed, so when you do appear before her, you must guard yourself accordingly. She will sense deceit and she will call you on it."

"How long have you been watching her?"

"She has been on my radar since childhood, but it is only in the last few years that I have come to learn as much as I have about her and know with certainty that she is the one made for me."

"You never really explained all of that to me. How is she the one when there are so many others to choose from? Why is she even human at all? I would expect someone with your level of expertise to want something a little more, I don't know, experienced."

"You have much to learn, Ryan. While I may enjoy the sexual as it pertains to the feed, in other facets of my existence it is the farthest thing from my mind. I do not want this being in that way. I want her to rule Hell with me and in the end, with us. She is made of Heaven, which means there can be no other."

I still don't see how this girl can be the one, but since I'm not the one that wants to marry her and in the end have her by my side as we rule together, it's not up to me to understand. It's only up to me to bring her to him when she's ready to accept what her destiny is.

"That is something else you must know."

"Which is?"

"It is not only her destiny that this will affect."

"Who else could there be?"

"Ryan, it is not only Serenity's destiny, but yours as well. The two of you will do this together."

My path is clear. I have to go into this with the mindset that I will succeed and I will bring the woman Lucifer wishes to claim as his own back to him. To his side where she will take her rightful place and aide in the destruction of the world as we know it.

There can be no failure.

In the same way I completed every task leading up to this point, I will do so again once he has given me the go ahead to start. He says there is still much to prepare as it pertains to the girl we are now watching so intently, so there is still some time where I must return to the way I have been and await further word from him.

This time, it's something I can do easily because I know everything now. There are no more secrets between us. I know why he did all of the things he has done with me, the reasons why he felt he had to do them and what he wants for me and us in the future.

For the next six months, I will go through the motions as I have done before. I will count down the days and when he comes to me again, I will be ready.

"You are aware of what you must do now."

"I am, Father."

"When I leave today, I will return exactly six months to the very minute and there will be no time for conversation. You will have had to adapt during my time away because any time wasted will bring out an ending that I am just not prepared to face."

"I know. I will be ready when you call."

"Serenity Richards is unlike any other human you have ever encountered and she is the very reason that I had to test you the way I did with Ava. If she was unable to break you then I can be sure that whatever does take place between you and Serenity, she will be unable to do so as well."

"What is it about her that makes you believe I would break? You've seen the way I've been. It's highly unlikely it will ever happen, least of all with a girl as plain as she is."

"It is always the ones you least expect that manage to take your breath away, Ryan. Remember that as we forge ahead. Serenity may look plain, but she is far more than that and I am sure that once you experience her for yourself the way that I have, you will see where my concerns lie."

"You have nothing to worry about, Father. Just as in times past, I have no interest in doing anything but serving you and making sure you achieve all that you so richly deserve. I will go to my grave in order to make it happen."

"Let us hope it does not come to that."

*****

Everything that's happened in my life has been leading up to this moment. All of the abuse, the darkness, the true agony I experienced as I walked this wretched life alone, my prayers unanswered and my anger growing, it all led me to where I stood watching Serenity.

Lucifer wanting more for me then to live life squatting away, no better than the homeless people he passes on the street every time he allows himself to come topside, manipulated time and space and set me up in an apartment a few short minutes from the Stephenville campus.

He made it quite clear that no matter how bad the urges became, or how much I wanted to jumpstart his plan, I had to remain in my location, going about my life but keeping myself at a comfortable distance at all times from Serenity or anyone that surrounded her. While I wasn't a fan of the place he chose, feeling that I could have done just as well in a smaller place, I didn't fight against what he'd given me.

There would be a time in the not so distant future where I would make my way to the campus and immerse myself in the student way of life again, but until that moment arose, I was determined to do as I had always done. Roam the world, unbeknownst to others, cloaked in the darkness of the night, finding willing participants and taking what I needed from them, leaving them bloodied, bruised and broken. I would do it all with a smile on my face, holding onto the knowledge that even though for a short time I had been swayed by the demon known as Ava, I would not be again.

Lucifer was none the wiser to my tricks as I continued to block him, determined then to do it until such time as he came to terms with the way he made me and let me handle myself in whatever way I wanted.

He believed me to be an abomination and he wasn't wrong. I am the worst of the worst and nothing, not even him, will keep me from embracing that which he believes me to be.

There is an excitement building inside me now.

I cannot wait until I turn twenty-one because that will be the day my life truly begins. The time where the darkness, which has been hidden and looked down upon for so very long, will finally break through and triumph over the light.

Chapter Thirteen
Darkness and Light Collide

This had to be the worst way to spend a birthday and considering the way the rest of mine had gone over the years, that's saying something.

Entering Stephenville Community College and signing up for classes, appearing to be a regular student like the rest of the useless humans was the last thing I wanted to be doing on my birthday, but there was no turning back.

The excitement I had leading up to this moment had faded over the six month wait and despite still wanting to see it through to the end the way I did before, I'd rather it be happening anywhere but where it had to.

Sensing my feelings on the matter, with me not shutting them down in time, Lucifer made it quite clear that in order for the plan to move along, this is where I needed to be, regardless of what day it was.

According to him, birthdays were meaningless anyway. At least they were when it came to what I truly am.

Celebrating the way you were brought into the world for most people is an elaborate affair. It's the day the light was shone on you in all its glory and you were sent to make your mark. It's not that way for me because the day I was forced into this meaningless existence, there had been no light.

Only darkness.

A darkness that I embraced fully and was guided by. It's that darkness that put the plan I had to execute in motion, and it's that darkness that will bring about the end for all the humans I now encounter flittering around me.

I had one purpose. To find the angelic ball of light and grow close to her. Preparing her for her rightful place beside Lucifer.

He was to take her as his bride, syphoning all the power she holds so tightly inside until his final act can commence.

The truth is, until I got to the campus, I'd been looking forward to this assignment. Learning that the target is a girl the same age as me, one that experiences the same things I do because of what she really is underneath the human disguise, had given me a level of excitement I haven't experienced in years. If there's one thing I've learned over the years, human girls are easy to manipulate. Even if Serenity Richards is different and not entirely human, I have no doubt she will be easy as well.

After the one experience with Ava, I had sworn off women forever. It was only because of Lucifer and what he wanted to accomplish that I was willing to step out of my self-imposed box. I would use what had been given to me, both in looks and charisma and I would bring Serenity Richards to her knees with the force of it.

Well I would have been able to do that if the dean hadn't spent the majority of the morning hidden behind his closed office door, preventing me from moving the plan along faster.

Serenity is unaware of it, but when I arrived here in the early hours of the morning, I saw her and the blonde sitting in the middle of the quad. I was quite a distance away, but even from afar, I could see what it is about her that Lucifer finds so enchanting. Her hair is long and wavy, flowing down her back in a way I can only describe as magical, and her body, while curvy fills out evenly with her average height. What was most important though and was the entire reason for my being there was the light that surrounded her.

Seeing that, there is no doubt that she is born of Heaven. It wasn't a bright light because she hadn't realized what she was and what flows so deeply through her body and from her very soul, but what was visible was enough to let me know why this girl had to be the one.

From my vantage point, I had been able to hear their conversation and while to others it may have seemed like a normal conversation, to me it was so much more. I was able to learn so much about her from the brief interaction, both in the way she spoke, the words that were said and her mannerisms.

Making what may possibly have been an arduous task, amazingly simple.

*****

"Remind me again why I agreed to do this with you?"

"Because you're still trying to talk me out of my major?"

"You gotta admit, Ser, after the center, this is the last thing you should be doing."

"What if I want to do things differently than they did, Ems? What we went through isn't the way things are everywhere. Wanting to be a doctor and help people doesn't have to be a bad thing."

"Not if you're dealing with people that have the same problems as you do."

"Thanks for the reminder. I'd almost gone a whole ten minutes not thinking about the fact that I can hear dead people."

"I don't mean it like that, Ser. I just—I want to make sure you know what you're getting into. It's the whole reason I agreed to transfer into this class with you."

"You want to change my mind, you mean."

"I guess I do. Look, if I wanna make sure I get to class, I need to go see the dean now. With as much time as I've spent in his office lately, I know that if I don't go now, it will take another week before you see me again."

She laughs and the sound seems to almost attach itself to me as I listen in, until it's all I can hear from all directions. Shaking off the feeling, watching as the best friend stands from her spot on the grass and makes her way toward the building I'm now standing in front of, I realize its show time.

The in that I need with Serenity. I've found it.

*****

It's the friend that's in the office with the dean and who is keeping me from the task at hand. If I didn't need her in order to gain access to Serenity, I would find a way to end her the minute she exited the room. The reality is, she is an integral part of what has to happen next, so for the time being, she has to remain alive.

As the door to the office opens and they make their way out into the hall, I catch her eye and doing my best to appear normal, I motion toward the man behind her and smirk. It's better to get her on my side now, than to let the opportunity pass by. She is needed after all.

Returning the smirk with one of her own, I stand and move forward, stopping when I reach the man and extending my hand. As he slaps his own into it, I meet his eyes, making sure all traces of the smirk are gone and that my face is a mask of nothingness.

"You must be Ryan." He states and after getting my confirmation as I nod, he continues. "I received your paperwork this morning. I appreciate the time taken to make sure everything needed was attached."

"My pleasure, sir. Anything to make the adjustment easier."

"It would appear that we don't need to meet the way I assumed when I spoke to you last week, so you're free to head to your classes now. Have you received the course schedule?"

"Yes sir."

"Ms. Daniels can show you where your classes are located. I do believe it's the least she can do." He offers as his eyes finally leave me and land straight on Emma, who looks put out at the mere thought of helping me figure out where I need to be.

"Yeah, sure. Of course." She says, though they're laced with sarcastic undertone.

Yes, I most definitely need to find a fitting end to this girl once my time with her is through. The annoyance may be leveled toward the man standing in front of us, but she has no idea who I am and the level of disrespect she's showing in my presence. It's upsetting. Given the way girls have been with me for the last ten years, I find it hard to believe this one is not as taken with me as she should be.

Her not giving me the desired reaction makes her expendable.

Motioning toward the door, leveling Emma with a look that I can only describe as one of warning, the dean turns on his heel and goes back into his office, shutting the door behind him and leaving us completely alone.

"So what's your first class?" Emma asks, her voice lighter than it had been seconds before and in getting a full view of her, I can now see why that is.

Where before I had assumed she had no reaction to me, I'd been wrong. She's now clearly taking me in and realizing what before had gone unnoticed. The way she seems to look through me, her eyes rising and falling in a matter of seconds, reminds me of the girls in school before Lucifer came for me.

She's definitely interested.

Too bad for her that she's the last person I would ever be interested in. I had gotten to see enough of her around campus since my arrival and her bubbly nature makes me long for the torture chambers of Hell.

"Psychology. Can't remember the professor's name."

She laughs and it makes my head hurt. The sound is as shrill as nails on a chalkboard. Humans never cease to grate on what is left of my nerves. I know I'm one of them, at least in part, but in the times when I've interacted with others, I don't sound or act like any of them and I prefer it that way.

"That's where I'm heading. Come on, we're already late as it is."

As we walk across the campus, she tells me about herself and I do my best to sound interested, but it's when she brings up Serenity that I really become involved. According to her, she has been sitting in on the class for days to be with her friend even though she'd been late multiple times, and just as I heard outside earlier, the only reason she's there at all is so that Serenity doesn't have to be alone.

It intrigues me, the way she speaks of Serenity and loneliness. From what I've been told of the girl and even experienced myself, it does appear as though her gifts have made her something of a social pariah, which is something I can identify with.

Maybe Emma Daniels isn't expendable after all. Where I may have issues breaking through to the ball of light, I can always come back and bother her in order to get close again. As irritating as her bubbly and talkative personality can be, there is no doubt that right now she is my biggest asset.

Making our way into the building and stopping at the first door on the right, she turns to me and pointing toward the door she speaks.

"Are you ready?"

"As ready as I can be considering it's school."

"You sound as thrilled to be here as I do."

We seem to agree on something after all. We may not like school or classes for the same reasons, but it's apparent by her rigid posture that this is definitely the last place she wants to be.

"Just wanna get this over with. My dad wanted me to come here for school, so I'm doing it. Doesn't mean I have to like it."

"Exactly." Emma agrees before pushing her way through the doors with me following directly on her heels.

Entering the room, the professor turns and there can be no mistaking the scowl that takes over his entire face. What Emma said earlier must be true. Her lateness is causing issues. As she begins to speak to him, I allow my eyes to wander and once they go all the way to the back, I spot my reason for being here.

With the distance, I'm not sure she's even able make me out, but there's no mistaking as her eyes come to rest at the front of the room that I've noticed her. Just as she appeared outside earlier, she looks now. As captivating as ever, her heavenly light glowing under the fluorescent lights of the classroom.

It's show time. The beginning stages of Lucifer's plan are about to begin.

It's time for me to meet Serenity Richards.

Chapter Fourteen
When Your Heart Stops Beating

After listening to the Professor berate Emma for her lateness, we did as he said and made our way to the back of the room, where she threw herself into the seat behind Serenity and I took the one to her left.

The entire walk up the aisle I'd been watching her, though I'd done my best not to appear as though I was. Anytime it seemed as though she might lift her head in my direction and lock eyes with me, I would look around the rest of the room so that she would be none the wiser to my interest in her.

I had a blueprint that I needed to follow and freaking the girl out before I had the chance to get close was not going to be a part of it. I would make Serenity Richards come to me, but only on her own timetable. Not a second before.

As I take my seat, I feel her eyes on me, but instead of reaching out the way I want and looking at her again, I stare straight ahead and listen as her obnoxious friend begins speaking again.

"So what did we miss?" she asks and as always, the experience of nails across a board comes over me, my blood pressure rising and making me want to cover my ears. As I am about to cave in and do exactly that, Serenity, who up until now I have avoided even acknowledging speaks and instantly, my mind is completely at peace.

There's a buzzing sound present when she talks, but not one I'm put off by. In fact, the way it seems to numb all of my other senses is pleasant. I'm not familiar with whatever it is, but it's something I can see being quite useful during our time together if it is indeed something she's creating.

Could her power somehow be aware of my own and this is the reaction that occurs when it happens?

It's something I definitely need to look into the minute we get out of here. If it's something that's going to occur frequently, I want to know all I can about it.

"Not much. He was just breaking down one of aspects we'll be studying over the next couple weeks."

"So I could have just stayed in bed?" I interject, knowing it's not my place, but unable to stop the pull I seem to experience sitting this close and listening to her. All attempts at being able to keep my focus elsewhere seem to be failing and in an effort to adapt, I give in to what it appears my mind and body want most.

Her.

Serenity's eyes are locked on me, as mine are to her and its being this close that I'm now able to see everything that the distance between us before had left me unable to. Her eyes are hazel, almost bordering on brown and they seem to play nicely off of the shading of her hair, which is now pinned back behind her ears with a clip.

With my enhanced ability, I can feel her quickened heart pumping away in her chest and can even make out the faint line of sweat beginning to appear at the base of her neck.

She's affected by me. Despite feeling her eyes inspecting me, my gaze falls to her lips, full and pouty, unlike others I've encountered as they are bare of any trace of makeup.

I sense the intake of breath before I hear it and despite wanting to keep my abilities hidden, I cannot help but smirk at the sound. She may be made of Heaven, have power like none other before her, but she is still very much human and her reaction to me confirms it. She's attracted even though she doesn't want to be.

Pulling away from her lips and again raising my eyes to meet her own, I'm struck by what happens the second I do. My breath hitches in my throat so tight that I find it almost impossible to breathe. Her eyes. It's as though she is privy to my every thought with how completely she seems to see through me. I begin to wonder if she is more aware of her abilities then Lucifer let on.

For me to have a reaction as strong as this, there must be more going on. Her head dips to the side in confusion at what I can only assume is the look I'm giving her now and I do my best to shake off my reaction.

I need to keep a level head if I'm to see this through the way Lucifer wants. I cannot let whatever I'm experiencing override the end game. This is not about my very human reaction to the ball of light sitting across from me, but about what she will mean, not only to me, but Lucifer and the world when the undertaking is complete.

"Ryan McGregor." I say, forcing my voice to remain as neutral as possible as I stick my hand out across the space between us. Just what I'm doing handling it this way is beyond me, but my move, it seems to have had an equally disconcerting effect on her.

Maybe now she can begin to experience what I did in looking at her. I for one do not want to be alone in whatever this is.

She is staring at my hand now, sizing it up much the same way she did to my body earlier and I can see that she is locked on the ink that covers my arms. Wearing the hoodie the way I did today, was done to hide the very real markings that cover my body, but it appears as though it had not the job effectively as she's caught on to it.

Well Look here! I think I've died and gone to Heaven!"

It has been awhile since the voices have been loud enough for me to hear, and I can't say I've missed it, but it feels rather good to finally hear one again. In the moment I now find myself stuck in, the way I am drawn to Serenity, I welcome the interruption.

Doing as I have done countless times before, she shakes herself, completely unaware that I can hear the voice and she lifts her eyes to mine, her hand coming out in front of her and meeting mine in the middle of the lane.

The minute we connect, there's a current that runs from my fingertips all the way up my arm and despite the need to break away, I remain locked in place. Her heart now pumping faster than before, her eyes raising, there is no doubt that I'm not the only going through this.

What is this? Her heartbeat is joining with mine, the beats taking place at the same exact moment. We are connecting and for the first time since all of this started, it's freaking me out. I'm not supposed to be having this kind of reaction. She is to be Lucifer's bride and nothing more. A means to an end that I want to see take place. Not someone to which I can experience this level of comfort or calm with.

"Serenity Richards."

"It's very nice to meet you, Serenity."

As believable as I hope that sounds, using power in order to make it appear as though I'm not reacting to her touch the way I clearly am, it's obvious that it's too much for her as she releases my hand and turns back toward the front of the room, breaking the contact between us and leaving my feeling unusually lost in the process.

Watching her as she focuses all of her attention on the professor, I see the paper come over her shoulder and drop down onto the desk in front of her. Shaking off the residual tingle still running through me from our touch, I continue to watch as she opens it, writes back and sends it back behind her to where Emma is on the edge of her seat with need waiting.

"Hmm." I say to no one in particular. Her head lifts and again she turns toward me, her gaze again somehow seeing straight through me in a comfortable yet unfamiliar way. Smirking at her, she tips her head to the side again, which just widens my smile that much more.

"What?" she whispers and I just shake my head.

"Oh, it's nothing. I'm just really glad I didn't stay home today."

Much the way she did moments before, I let my statement fall and turn my head back to the front of the room. That has to be enough for now. There is a need inside me that is dangerously close to pushing me toward her in a way that I'm not ready for. A way that if taken too quickly could spell disaster for the entire undertaking. It is something I cannot allow.

Whatever this response is to the ball of light, I need to get it under control and tame it. As badly as I want to look at her, have her eyes locked on any part of me that she wishes to gaze at, I need to remain focused. Something tells me that if I don't, she is going to catch on rather quickly to the real reason I'm here and until I'm told otherwise, that can't happen.

Despite the way being in her company feels, bringing to life things I haven't felt since I was younger, I need to keep my distance.

There can be no denial that there is indeed something taking place between us. A feeling so powerful, it has the ability to be life altering. Even as I watch her interact with Emma, the barest of smiles tracing those perfectly full lips, I feel my heart doing something that it has only done mechanically since birth.

It's coming alive inside my chest with every breath she seems to take. In meeting Serenity Richards, taking her in, my reactions are becoming one with hers.

We are becoming one.

It's wrong of me to think and react this way, but I have to do it. What Lucifer wants me to do, I will still see through, but I'm determined to enjoy myself while it happens. Which means that instead of backing away from what's happening now, I need to embrace every second of it. I need to know more about what this is.

I can't let whatever this is fade away. I want more.

I want Serenity.

Chapter Fifteen
I'm Going Through Changes

The rest of the day once we've gone our separate ways seems to pass in a blur.

I can't deny that when class let out, I wanted Serenity to be the one to reach out and show me around. What took place during our short time together was not one sided. I knew she could feel it just as much as I could, despite my attempts not to let it get to me and by the end, when we were about to go in different directions, I had hope she would put me out of the misery I brought on myself and reach out.

That was not to be and instead I was stuck with Emma, though now that I had met the ball of light, my tolerance level seemed to be at an all-time high. Where before the girl had gotten to me and grated on my every last nerve, now her words were dulled, making her slightly more tolerable.

It was during that short walk together that she gave me what I didn't even realize at the time I'd been looking for. Handing me a slip of paper and watching as I opened it, catching the number written on the inside, she smiled the minute I looked back up at her, my face showing just the right amount of confusion needed to keep her oblivious.

*****

"What's this?"

"Serenity's number."

"Why would I want Serenity's number?"

"You're gonna tell me you weren't staring at her the entire class?"

Shit. I was busted.

"That obvious, huh?"

"Completely. I should probably warn you though, Serenity; she doesn't exactly do well with dating."

"What do you mean?"

"She's awkward with people. I probably shouldn't even give you the number, but honestly, I think she needs this."

Yes. Emma Daniels is coming in handy after all. She's giving me far more information than I expected about her best friend and despite saying I needed it in order to move forward with my plan to get close to her, I am finding it's also for a more personal reason.

"And if I don't wanna date her?"

"Well, I suppose the two of you can just be friends, but considering the way you looked at her in class, I think you not wanting her is crap."

"You might be right about that. I can't just call her and chat her up though."

"Ryan," she sighs. "Just call her. Say you need help with class or whatever. I'll deal with the rest."

For the first time since being in her company I'm thankful for the advice. Having no previous experience past what happened with Ava to guide me, any help in that department is appreciated. Asking her for help is definitely a way for me to get close to her, even if I don't very much care about the classes or passing them.

'Why are you doing this?"

"Because even though she won't admit it, Serenity is one of the loneliest people I know and even if she isn't big on the whole dating thing, she is with helping others and I think you two can help each other."

She has no idea how close she is to the truth. Serenity is definitely going to be helping in a very short amount of time. It might not be the way Emma means, but the minute I bring her to Lucifer, she will be helping the darkness achieve everything it has been trying to do for centuries.

"Well, umm—thanks I guess." I say, pocketing the number, not sure what else can be said now. I could easily tell her that I would

*call Serenity and set things up and be everything her friend needs
and more, but that would be a lie and I can't bring myself to do it.*

*For the first time in what feels like forever, lying is the last
thing I want to do, with the best friend or even with Serenity
herself.*

What has gotten into me?

*****

It's been a few hours since that conversation and here I am
in my room, staring at the paper with her number on it, the
phone in my hands, willing my fingers to just do what should
come easily and call the girl.

Emma had already given me all that I needed in order to
move the plan along and get to know her. Now all I had to do was
get up the nerve to use it.

I don't do things like this. *Shit*. It's so awkward that it's
actually making me feel like I wanna throw up. I might look a
certain way, have confidence because of my power, but that
doesn't mean squat when dealing with humans. I'm not a
romantic, in fact I don't think I believe in love at all anymore, but
now here I am expected to act as though I do.

Calling her, I want to do it. I want to hear her voice on the
other end of the line, no matter how put off she may be by me
calling. I want to hear her breathing, imagining as I do the way
her lips will purse in annoyance, the pouty look from earlier that
much more prominent.

Serenity Richards is doing what no other person or being
before her could do and she is completely unaware of it. One
touch from her, one look and I have been completely consumed.
If this is what Lucifer experienced during his times keeping tabs
on her, then it's no surprise that he wants her so badly. I haven't
even made the call yet and I already want to make her mine.

It's disconcerting. I'm doing exactly what he feared I would
do. I am allowing my human way of being override the task at
hand. Continuing this will only spell disaster.

Which only makes me want to call her even more.

Picking up the phone and pressing in the numbers written on the paper, I wait as I hear the rings go in, becoming more impatient with each passing one that goes ignored.

As I'm about to give up and push to end the call, I hear her voice and despite my best attempts at blocking it out, my body instantly reacts as my heart begins to speed up and a warmth previously unknown completely envelopes my body.

"Hello?"

"Yeah—umm—is Serenity there?"

She's only said hello and already my mouth is beginning to dry up and I'm struggling not to choke. What the hell is it about this girl that has me losing my nerve so quickly?

"This is her."

"Oh! Hey! It's Ryan, you know—umm—from class."

Real smooth McGregor. Why don't you stumble over every word a little more? I'm sure the nervousness is a turn on.

"Yeah, I know who you are, Ryan. What can I do for you?"

"Well you know, I'm new and I'm two weeks behind. I was hoping that if you could spare the time, you would help me catch up in some of the classes we have in common."

I hear a voice in the background, one I can only assume is Emma and then I hear Serenity though she's slightly more muffled than before. Because of my hearing being stronger, I hear what she hisses out to Emma and I can't help smiling. She wasn't lying earlier. Serenity really doesn't do anything remotely social well.

I don't want to, but I can't help it. I find her cute. This girl, she's endearing.

It's only when I hear a scuffle and Emma's voice comes across the line that everything I felt up until that point fades away. As tolerable as I've been with her, she's not the one I need to get close to.

"Hey Ryan, its Emma. Serenity says she'd love to get together with you. Just text her the details of when and where and she'll be there."

"Sorry about that, she took the phone from my hands." Serenity says, again throwing my body into a tailspin at the sound of her voice.

"No problem. Was she right though? I mean, would you like to get together? You'd be doing the world a great favor by helping out one of your fellow students. You might even end up with your name on a park bench someday."

A park bench? Is that the best I can come up with? Geez, I need to get out more. I suck at this.

Before I can berate myself more, I hear her laugh and just as quickly as it comes, it's muffled again. It's as if she caught herself laughing and tried to stop it. Strange, but another thing I'm familiar with. It's just another way we're alike.

"I doubt that, but sure. We can get together and go over what you might need extra help with."

"Yes!" I shout, not sure where the exuberance comes from but running with it. "Thank you. You really are a life saver, Serenity."

Grabbing a pen when she mentions taking down her number, I listen intently as she says the numbers slowly, repeating them back to her once she's done so I know I've got the right sequence, giving her mine in the same way until we've said all there is to say.

Wanting the conversation to continue yet not having the first clue what to say in order to make it happen, proving again just how crappy I am at this, I breathe a sigh into the phone and prepare myself for the goodbye that's coming.

"I'll text you in the morning about a time to meet up, okay?" she asks and I nod, wanting to slap myself the minute I do for not realizing that she can't see it.

Man, this is not going the way I pictured it at all.

"Yeah, that sounds great. I'll talk to you later, pretty girl."

Pushing the end call button, I throw the phone down on the bed and sigh even louder than I did on the phone. What the hell did I just call her and better yet, why did I call her it?

When Lucifer gets wind of this, I'm gonna be a dead demon walking.

*****

When I got up in the morning I saw she texted, having passed out long before I heard from her the night before and responded back right away, setting up a time for the late afternoon after our classes, when we would actually be free to spend more than a few seconds together.

I know it's wrong, considering that for me there is more going on than just the mission Lucifer tasked me with, but I can't stop it. I want to spend time with this girl, even if I have to risk my own existence to do it. As enticing as the position in Hell is, there is something even more so about her, and I can't back away until I figure it out.

It's only when I walk into Intro to Biology, the one class I thought I wouldn't see her that I'm taken aback to see her sitting in the front row, her lips lifting into a smile the minute she spots me.

"Holy shit! You're in this class too?"

"Looks like it. I guess I know what you're going to need to be caught up in."

Sliding myself into the seat beside her, I turn my body to get a better look, hoping that she won't notice the once over I seem to be giving her body and it occurs to me that today, instead of having her hair pulled back the way it was yesterday, it's loose and the waves are more prominent. If I wasn't attracted to her before, it's hard not to be now. She's gorgeous in a subtle, breath of fresh air kind of way.

Mesmerizing.

Breathtaking and most definitely perfect for Lucifer.

"Uggh."

"That's a promising sound, considering the class hasn't even started yet."

In an attempt to hide my thoughts from her even though it appears as though she doesn't share my ability to be able to read them, I come up with an excuse for the moan I just let escape. Laughing in an attempt to throw her off, I say the first thing that comes to mind even though it has nothing to do with the thoughts I was having seconds before.

"I was going to ask you something, but no matter how I say it, it's gonna sound like a line."

"Hey sexy, what's your major?"

The way she comes back so easily with the response makes me think I need to focus more on the whole mind reading thing after all. It seems she catches on a little too quickly, which right now is the last thing I need even though what's happening between us is still fairly innocent.

"Yeah that's the one. You nailed it. Though if I said it, it would have been a little different."

"How so?"

Leaning across my seat, so close to her that I can see the breath escaping from my lips making her hair move just slightly, I whisper and with the shiver that comes from my words, I'm satisfied that I've hit my mark. Maybe I don't suck at this after all.

I like the way her shiver makes my body feel.

"So beautiful, what do you want to be when you grow up?"

Moving back comfortably into my seat, I watch her react to what I've done. Her cheeks are now flushed pink and I'm pretty sure if I reached out to touch her in the moment, I would find her body heated the same way mine is.

There is no doubt about it now, there is definitely something between Serenity and me, and I've never been so eager to find out what.

"Well, isn't he a delicious morsel of a man! The things I would let him do to me!"

"You could just eat off that chest! Whatever that smell is coming off of him, it's heavenly."

"Go away!" she says, her voice obviously irritated yet low enough that I almost don't catch it.

She's heard the voices and it's obvious now, when she is doing everything in her power to appear like every other girl on campus, she's not enjoying it for a second.

What she doesn't realize is, I know all about her supposed disability and it's one of the things that is supposed to bond us, though with the way I've been reacting to her since we met a little over twenty-four hours ago, we're already a lot more bonded then I realized.

Seeing her irritation and then the fear that comes across her face, I want to reach out and tell her that it's okay. It's totally against protocol and the reason for me being here, but I don't want this girl believing for a second that she's alone in this. Crude as that last one may have been, I can hear them too and there's no reason in the world she needs to hide from it or be ashamed of my reaction.

"What's that?"

"Huh?"

"You said something. I thought maybe you said it to me." I say, hoping that now is the time she'll admit what's going on, but instinctively knowing it won't be the case. Serenity will keep this close to the vest, the same way I did for so long.

"I didn't say anything, maybe you just wanted me to."

"Touché." I respond with a smile. "You might be right about that." At the last second I decide to try something I've never done and I wink. It's then I'm rewarded. She freezes in place and blushes. Not wanting to push anything further, I turn away and give her a chance to right herself.

When I'm sure she's had enough time to adjust, I lean back over and in the smallest voice I can manage, do the one thing that until now I'd been determined not to. I tell her the truth.

"It's okay," I whisper. "I hear them too."

There's definitely no doubt about it. I like this girl and worse, I'm starting to think that what Lucifer wants with her, really isn't the right thing after all.

Epilogue
Absence of Light

What most people don't realize is, I fell in love with her the moment her ability became exposed to me.

People believe that love can't happen quickly. That what one person feels when they first meet someone they're attracted to is just a release of a high level of endorphins, or lust and that they just mistake it for love.

They're wrong.

I knew sitting in that biology class that Serenity Richards was the one. I also knew that she was the one I prayed for. The one I mistakenly thought Jackson was when I was younger. The way she reacted, it said a lot about who she is. How alike we really are and by the time the class was over and we were on our way for coffee, I knew I wanted to make her mine.

There's no one in the world meant for me other than her. It's what makes her being gone now so fucking hard. I can't seem to breathe without her.

That's what she was to me that first day and I think that's what she'll always be. The air I need to continue moving on despite who and what I am and the horrific life I've led.

Things are different now. I'm not just a demon hybrid anymore. I'm a whole lot more than that, but none of it matters for shit if she's not here. I don't want to be an angel when the only real angel I've ever known and cared about has been ripped away from me.

I don't want to function at all.

She knew I was different. That first day when I thought she was looking through me, it's because she was. She looked into the darkest parts of me and found the light. She brought it out of me and now that it's here, despite how driven by the demonic I still am, she's not here to see just how much it's changed me.

For so long I believed that Lucifer was the one that would save me from the horrible life I'd been living. He would be the one to rescue me from Corinne and bring me into something that in the end would give my life real purpose. I would finally feel alive for the first time since my very creation, but it wasn't him at all.

Yes, for a time I found my life had purpose with him, but not in the way I wanted it to be. He couldn't give me that because he wasn't capable of it. All he could see was how wrong everything was instead of looking deeper and seeing that everything was right and he was the one that was wrong.

Serenity is the one that gave me purpose and I will not rest until I find her and bring her back.

She might believe me to be better than I've been all this time, but I'm nothing without her. I might have the light inside me, I might even be a pure angel the way the others claim, but without her, that light is dimmed and purity is an unattainable dream.

I need her here so that when I become the man she always knew I could be, she can see that what I told her before is true. She is my dream come true, my answered prayer and she is in everything from the air surrounding me, to what lies below me.

She is in all of it because she is all of it.

Serenity Richards is everything and if she would just come back to me, all of the horrible things I've done in my past, everything I've been sitting here over the last few days and remembering, could all be erased. I could be the person she believes I was meant to be. The one worthy of redemption and not the dark and broken mess that my time with Lucifer helped me become.

Al of the pain and agony that during a few short years of time I unleashed on a world that I thought deserved it, could be made right again, or at least with her by my side I would be able to at least begin the process of making it right, even if it takes me the rest of my life to achieve it.

The longer she's gone though, the more my past; everything I've done and lived through threatens to control me. The scent of the blood, the taste of the flesh when I buried my teeth into it, along with the pleasure that came from hurting people, it's all still there just dying to get out and I'm so damn scared that if she doesn't come back, I'm going to break and when I do, the way I was will have its way with the person I'm attempting to become.

I'm not Ryan McGregor, the human anymore. I'm not even the demon hybrid.

Until she's returned and I can feel her essence again, have it completely invade my senses and turn what's twisted, right again, there is only one thing I will be and that is nothing at all.

The light will always win over the darkness, I know that to be true, but right now with the loss I feel inside, the torturous way my thoughts and my past seem to be conspiring against me, it won't be long until what I believe changes and I live forever in the dark.

Without Serenity, I'm living in a world that's absent of light and I've never be so scared in my life.

The End

Absence of Light Playlist

Wayward One by Alter Bridge
Breath by Breaking Benjamin
On My Own by Ashes Remain
For Those Who Wait by Fireflight
The Story by Thirty Seconds To Mars
Save Me by Remy Zero
Bleed For Me by Saliva
Familiar Taste of Poison by Halestorm
All I Need To Be by Fireflight
Fall Apart by Earshot
Raining (feat. Adam Gontier) by Art Of Dying
Monster by Meg & Dia
Angel Eyes (feat. Chris Motionless) by New Years Day
Letters To God by Boxcar Racer
Do Your Worst by New Years Day
Hold Me, Thrill Me, Kiss Me, Kill Me by U2
The Kill by Thirty Seconds To Mars
Good Enough by Evanescence
Fading by Decyfer Down

Acknowledgements

This book and all that's contained in it wouldn't have been written if it wasn't for the people that bought and read the Love United Series and came back to me with their honest thoughts and at times even fan girl reactions. So the first acknowledgement I have to do is to all of you. Thank you for loving Ryan and this series as a whole as much as I do and wanting just a little bit more.

Joey Winchester, my beta-reader who over time turned into my co-author on a couple of books (one released and one to come). When I finished this story eight months ago and debated whether or not to release it to the world based on content, you were the one that told me to go for it because the world needed to know Ryan's story. This exists now because of that, and you. So thank you. Words will never express what your support, criticism and love mean to me. Love your face pretty boy and it's an always and forever kind of thing.

If I didn't thank this lady, this entire section wouldn't feel right. Pamela Sparkman, for continuing to be my champion, my friend, my beta-reader and my fan both in life and writing, I love and appreciate you. The stories I've written over the last year would not be what they are without you. I am blessed and honored to know an author as talented as you and a person as pure of heart as you. Thank you for being on this wonderfully crazy journey with me,

To any person out there that spends even five seconds with something I've written. Whether you found me through the Count On Me series or you came onto the crazy train at the beginning with Love United Series, I love all of your faces. I would not be doing what I am right now if it wasn't for you, truly. The chance you take spending hard earned money on something that's poured out of my mind and onto the pages means the absolute world and I will never forget any of you. Good or bad. I appreciate and love you all.

About The Author

Melyssa Winchester is a mother of four from Toronto, Ontario, Canada. When she's not knee deep in adolescent awesomeness, she's falling in love, one book boyfriend and girlfriend at a time. She is a lover of all things romance and will forever believe in a real and true happily ever after.

When she's not off being a mom or writing you can find her doing one of two things. Reading or buried under the covers watching Supernatural, Sons of Anarchy or Veronica Mars. Melyssa is currently working on **Through the Storm** (Count On Me #7) and **Unbreakable** (Tristan Reagan's story). In addition, she is also working on the standalone title **Remembering Sunday.** There also might be another heavenly adventure in the works, as only one of the fallen can bring.

You can find her on the web, either at her personal site, Facebook (which she just might have an obsession with) or Twitter (@WinchesterBooks) where she talks incessantly about her kids, her writing and all things book boyfriend related.

* 9 7 8 1 9 2 8 1 3 9 1 5 7 *